Jillian threw a snowball at him, but he dodged it.

"You know this means war," Miles said.

"Naturally."

She pulled her hand from behind her back and sent another snowball whizzing in his direction. In one smooth move, he ducked out of the way, dropped down, scooped up some snow and then charged her. She pelted him with snowballs, but he kept coming. They were laughing while they made and threw snowballs as fast as they could, getting closer and closer. When they were mere inches apart, he grabbed her around the waist, keeping her in place when she tried to escape.

"Oh no you don't." He held a gloveful of snow up to her face.

Her eyes widened. "You wouldn't dare."

"Think not?"

Their chests rose and fell as they took deep, gulping breaths. They were so close that their breaths mingled. Puffs of air escaped her slightly parted lips. There was a pink tinge to her cheeks and nose. She'd never been more beautiful.

The urge to kiss her was strong and suddenly he couldn't think of a good reason not to.

"So does this mean you give?" Jillian asked when he didn't move.

Dear Reader,

Welcome to Aspen Creek, Colorado, a resort/ranching community in the Rockies. This small town is the setting for my brand-new Aspen Creek Bachelors series. The skies are clear, the view is scenic and the air is filled with love.

Miles Montgomery and Jillian Adams are first on deck in *Valentines for the Rancher*. Theirs is a second-chance romance. Miles and Jillian had been friends from childhood. They dated all through high school and their early twenties. Jillian had been expecting an engagement ring, but Miles wanted to take a break. They went their separate ways, and each had a marriage that ended in divorce.

Now Jillian is back in Aspen Creek with her two-year-old daughter. Although Jillian plans to keep away from Miles and his three-year-old son, she and Miles are repeatedly thrown together. Add in the fact that her daughter and his son absolutely adore each other, and it's nearly impossible for her to stick to her plan.

I hope you enjoy *Valentines for the Rancher* as much as I enjoyed writing it.

Happy reading!

Kathy

Valentines
for the Rancher

KATHY DOUGLASS

HARLEQUIN
SPECIAL
EDITION

ISBN-13: 978-1-335-72447-2

Valentines for the Rancher

Copyright © 2023 by Kathleen Gregory

For questions and comments about the quality of this book, please contact us at CustomerService@Harlequin.com.

Harlequin Enterprises ULC
22 Adelaide St. West, 41st Floor
Toronto, Ontario M5H 4E3, Canada
www.Harlequin.com

Printed in U.S.A.

Recycling programs for this product may not exist in your area.

Kathy Douglass is a lawyer turned author of sweet small-town contemporary romances. She is married to her very own hero and mother to two sons who cheer her on as she tries to get her stubborn hero and heroine to realize they are meant to be together. She loves hearing from readers that something in her books made them laugh or cry. You can learn more about Kathy or contact her at kathydouglassbooks.com.

Books by Kathy Douglass

Harlequin Special Edition

The Fortunes of Texas: The Wedding Gift

A Fortune in the Family

Montana Mavericks:
The Real Cowboys of Bronco Heights

In the Ring with the Maverick

Furever Yours

The City Girl's Homecoming

Montana Mavericks: What Happened to Beatrix?

The Maverick's Baby Arrangement

Aspen Creek Bachelors

Valentines for the Rancher

Visit the Author Profile page
at Harlequin.com for more titles.

This book is dedicated to Angela Anderson
of Angela Anderson Presents,
Shay Baby of Brown Book Series
and Keisha Mennefee of Honey Magnolia PR.
Thank you for all that you have done for me
in particular and romance authors in general.
You ladies are making it happen.

This book is also dedicated with love
to my own personal heroes, my husband and
my two sons. Thank you for your love and support.
It means the world.

Chapter One

Jillian Adams lowered her car window, letting in the fresh mountain air. Although it was quite cold, she took a deep breath, inhaling the familiar scents before pressing the button and raising the window. After three years of living in Kansas City, Kansas, it felt good to be back in Aspen Creek, Colorado. Just seeing the soaring pine trees and snow-covered Rockies confirmed that she'd done the right thing by returning home.

"It won't be long now, Lilliana," she said. There was no reply from the backseat but she wasn't expecting one. At two years old, her daughter still fell asleep within minutes of getting in the car and generally didn't awaken until the ride ended. Back when Lilliana was a fussy newborn and Jillian had been an exhausted new mom, she'd started taking her daughter out on drives to get her to fall asleep. Even in those early days of parenthood, Evan couldn't be bothered to help care for his own child. Saying he needed his rest, he'd roll over in bed and go back to sleep. As if Jillian hadn't been run ragged from long hours at work, often feeling like she was on the verge of collapse. But Jillian would put Lilliana in her car seat and drive around until she nodded off.

Evan's attitude had been a clear sign that he didn't care a whit about Jillian or their child, but Jillian hadn't picked up on it. She'd been too busy caring for the baby and the house and working a full-time job to notice much of anything. As a result, she'd been blindsided five months ago when he'd told her that he wanted out of the marriage, dropped divorce papers on the kitchen table, grabbed his duffle and left.

Last month, she'd informed her landlord that she wouldn't be renewing her lease. She'd given notice at work, packed up her belongings, rented a trailer, gotten behind the wheel of her Ford Escape and hit the road. Her father and brothers had volunteered to help her move, but she'd turned them down. She needed to do this on her own, without inconveniencing anyone. Besides, she relished the time alone to think.

She'd learned several hard lessons over the past years, the main one being to listen to her brain and ignore her heart. Her heart had led her down the wrong road twice: first to her longtime boyfriend, Miles Montgomery, and then to Evan. Either her heart didn't have her best interest in mind, or it couldn't tell the right man from the wrong one. Either way, Jillian wasn't going to follow it again.

She wasn't interested in romance, anyway. She didn't have the time or energy to spend on love. All of her focus had to be on getting her life back on track and caring for her little girl. Although her parents had said she and Lilliana could stay with them as long as she'd like, Jillian intended for it to be a temporary arrangement.

The first thing she needed to do was get a job. That should be easy enough. She could return to her old job at her family's resort. Although Aspen Creek was known mostly for its skiing, snowmobiling and other outdoor winter activities, it was a destination twelve months of the year. In the off-season, vacationers came to enjoy the hiking, horseback riding, fishing and hot springs. As a result, the summer months were nearly as busy as the winter, so there would be plenty of work.

Jillian saw the exit sign for Aspen Creek and turned off the highway. Driving down the familiar roads brought back happy memories of times she'd spent with her friends. She passed the diner and smiled as she recalled the times she and her friends had spent there, eating burgers and milkshakes and talking about boys.

Her smile faded when she passed the Eating Is Believing seafood restaurant, the site of her last date with Miles Montgomery. The dinner that had ended it all. Despite the passage of time, her stomach seized, and she stepped on the gas, speeding past the restaurant. But it was too late. Despite telling herself the past was dead, the memory of her first romantic misadventure was there in living color.

Their mothers were best friends, so she and Miles had been close since childhood. They'd been high school sweethearts and they'd dated throughout college. Jillian had believed they were on their way to making a lifetime commitment, but he'd had plans that hadn't included her.

When Miles had told her he wanted to have a serious discussion, she'd bought a new dress and shoes and gotten her hair and nails done in anticipation of great things. She'd stepped into the restaurant believing that he was going to propose and that she would be going home engaged to the man she'd loved all her life. Instead he'd told her they needed to evaluate their relationship. They'd dated exclusively since they were fourteen—a total of nine years—and in his opinion they'd gotten serious too soon. She'd accused him of dating someone behind her back, something he'd denied. But he hadn't denied wanting to see other women, which in her mind was just as bad.

"And that's how I ended up with your daddy," Jillian said to her sleeping daughter. In retrospect, Evan had been her rebound guy. She'd just been too hurt to see it back then. Too determined to show Miles that she'd moved on, too. She'd tried to make the relationship into something it could never be. Even so, she couldn't regret their marriage because Lilliana, her greatest joy, had been the result.

Jillian drove the rest of the way to her parents' house, telling herself to stop brooding and to think positive thoughts. Her parents were thrilled she and Lilliana were moving home and she wasn't going to be a downer, moping around and showing everyone how hurt and confused she was. The last thing she wanted to do was be a Gloomy Gina and depress everyone. She was going to be Suzie Sunshine if it killed her. It shouldn't be hard to do given how often she'd pretended that everything in her marriage was fine. She couldn't count the number of times she'd pretended that Evan was a good husband, lying to her friends and coworkers. Lying to herself. She'd pasted on a smile, hoping that if she acted as if he was a devoted husband and father, he would magically morph into one. It hadn't worked.

She pulled onto the road leading past the resort and to her parents' house. Her paternal grandparents had built the resort over forty years ago. At the time, there had been only five small cabins and three slopes. Now there were over two hundred deluxe hotel rooms and suites. People came from far and near to enjoy the many amenities the Aspen Creek Resort provided.

Located in the mountains twenty-five minutes outside of town, the resort now occupied two hundred prime acres. Her family's house was on the land, as well, but far enough away from the resort for them to have privacy. Her parents had run the resort all of her life, although they'd begun stepping back, allowing Jillian's eldest brother, Grant, to take more control of the day-to-day operations.

Jillian took in the spectacular views before parking near the house. She'd barely gotten out of the car when the front door opened and her mother stepped onto the front porch. Her mother called over her shoulder for Jillian's father and then darted down the stairs. Valerie pulled Jillian into a strong embrace, rocking her back and forth, silently communicating that everything would be okay. Mom was here. Jillian closed her eyes and leaned into her mother's arms, basking in the warmth and comfort she found there.

After a few seconds, Jillian eased away and wiped a stray tear from her cheek. She wasn't a little girl any longer. Not only was she an adult, but she was a mother. She was the one who had to make everything okay for her own daughter. Lilliana was going to be counting on her for…well, everything. Although Evan deposited regular child support payments into Jillian's bank account, she hadn't heard a word from him since he'd left and didn't expect to. Three weeks ago, she'd had a lawyer review the divorce papers. Everything had been straightforward, so she'd signed where indicated and he'd filed the papers on her behalf. She'd received the final divorce decree two days ago, putting an end to her marriage.

"It's good to have you home," Valerie said. "Your room is all set for you. We moved a couple of pieces of furniture out to make room for Lilliana's crib. We figured with her being in a strange place, she'd feel more comfortable sharing a room with you for a while."

"That's fine. Thanks."

At that moment, Lilliana let out a loud cry. Jillian had been expecting it. Lilliana liked the motion of the car, but the minute it stopped she wanted out. Any delay would turn Jillian's ordinarily sunny child into a cranky toddler.

"Let me have a look at my grandbaby," Valerie said, opening the back door. She had Lilliana out of the car seat and in her arms before the child could get a good cry going. Valerie was an expert when it came to fussy children. She'd raised four kids all while helping to manage a successful business. She chucked Lilliana under her chin and then kissed her on her chubby cheek. Lilliana laughed gustily, clearly pleased to be in her grandmother's arms.

"Well, well, who do we have here?" Jillian's father said, jogging down the stairs.

"Daddy," Jillian said, rushing into her father's outstretched arms. She'd always been a daddy's girl, following her father around and getting dirtier than her three older brothers put together. Her brothers had teased her, calling her Pigpen after the Peanuts character who traveled with a cloud of dust wherever he went, but Henry had protected her.

"How's my little Jilly Bean?" Her father had been the first to call her that and it had stuck, becoming the family's nickname for her.

"Not so little anymore."

"Maybe not, but you're still my little girl. Now, let's get all this stuff unpacked and get you out of the cold. You'll need a few minutes to change before everyone gets here."

"Who's everyone and why are they coming here today?" It had been a long drive and she was looking forward to soaking in the tub and then enjoying a quiet night with her family.

"It's nothing big, so wipe that frown off your face before it freezes that way," her mother said as she climbed the stairs, Lilliana in one arm and the diaper bag thrown over the other. "It's just your brothers and some friends who want to stop by and say hello. So we're having a little gathering."

"Marty's manning the grill and Grant had a meeting he couldn't reschedule. Victor's shift at the fire department won't end for a while, so it's just the two of us moving in your stuff," her father added. Jillian inhaled and got a whiff of smoky charcoal and grilling meat that she hadn't noticed before.

Henry and Jillian began unloading the trailer, then followed Jillian's mother into the house. Valerie was in the process of putting a clean diaper on Lilliana when they stepped into the living room. Jillian preferred cloth diapers, using disposable ones only in emergencies. Her mother was holding a soaked cloth diaper in one hand while trying to hold a squirming Lilliana in place long enough to put a diaper on her bare bottom.

"I'll take that," Jillian said, putting down the boxes she was carrying and grabbing the wet diaper from her mother.

"Thanks. I never could get the hang of those things. Plastic tabs were so much easier."

Jillian dropped the soiled diaper into a bag she kept for just that purpose. "The plastic cover has Velcro so it's just as easy. All you do is put the diaper in and go."

Jillian exchanged places with her mother and in a few seconds, Lilliana was in a clean diaper. Jillian snapped the buttons on the pink corduroy pants with yellow butterflies and set her daughter on her feet again. Lilliana laughed and ran straight for her grandmother, who swooped her up. Seeing Lilliana bond with Valerie warmed Jillian's heart. Although she loved her parents, the distance between them and their busy schedules kept them from getting together as often as they would have liked. Jillian was thrilled that Lilliana would be close to her grandparents and uncles now.

Valerie kissed the baby's cheek. "Grandma made cookies."

"Mom," Jillian said.

"Don't start. She's in a new place. We want her to feel at home."

Jillian sighed. There was no sense in arguing over a treat. "Just one."

"Of course," Valerie said with a smile. "I don't want to spoil her dinner."

"No, you're just going to spoil the baby," Henry said.

Jillian laughed at the put-out expression on her mother's face. Jillian wasn't one for giving Lilliana too many treats, but she knew that food was her mother's favorite way of showing love. Valerie baked gorgeous birthday cakes from scratch for her family, made elaborate Sunday dinners and often sent baked goods to her friends when they were sick, or just because they were on her mind. Food was her love language and she spoke it fluently.

Truth be told, Lilliana could use all of the love she could get. They both could. These past months had been rough. Although Jillian realized she needed to stand on her own two feet, it was nice knowing that there were loving arms willing to uphold her—or even carry her—when she needed it.

Henry insisted on toting the heavy boxes, so Jillian grabbed a couple lighter ones and followed him to her room. It was sad to see just how little she owned. All her worldly possessions had fit in a rented trailer. But starting fresh would be easier without a bunch of reminders from the past, so she'd donated or given away quite a bit.

"I'll just leave the boxes here inside the door. You can put things wherever you want," her father said, going back downstairs to grab more of her belongings.

After two trips, everything was inside. He'd put the playpen and the boxes of Lilliana's toys in the family room and set the highchair in the kitchen. Jillian wasn't in the mood to unpack, so she headed outside to talk to her brother.

"Hey," she said, stepping onto the covered patio. "If it's not Party Marty."

"And Jilly Bean, together again," Marty said, reaching out to give her a big hug.

After embracing him, she stood back and gave her brother a close look. At twenty-nine, Marty was nearest to her in age and always up for anything. They'd once been partners in crime, getting into more than a little bit of trouble. Now he smiled broadly, a twinkle in his eyes. He might be on the verge of kissing the twenties goodbye, but there was still plenty of mischief in Marty.

"Need help?"

He shook his head. "Nah."

"Don't say I didn't offer." She draped a blanket over her shoulders and dropped into a comfortable chair in front of the firepit. She watched as her brother opened the enormous grill and turned the meat. There were several slabs of ribs cooking in indirect heat.

"This is the easy part. You should have been here when I was seasoning the chicken and steaks and doing the other prep work." He gestured at a pile of foil-wrapped potatoes on a tray near a smaller grill to be cooked later. A few dozen ears of corn were soaking in a huge pot of water. There was easily enough food for thirty people.

Jillian looked at the tent that had been set up at the edge of the lawn. It was enormous. A few workers were wheeling in round tables while others carried in chairs. "Just how big is this shindig? Mom said it was just family and a couple of close friends."

"You know Mom. She's never been good at math. Especially when it comes to counting friends."

"Yeah." Valerie had never met a stranger. To her, everyone was a potential friend. And good friends were soon counted as family.

"What time is this little party supposed to start?"

"Around five. So that leaves you plenty of time to shower and get into something nice. Maybe do something with your hair."

"What's wrong with the way I look?"

"Nothing if you're going for the bedraggled traveler look."

Jillian glanced at her clothes. She hated to admit it, especially to Marty, who as usual was impeccably dressed, but she was a mess. She'd packed the trailer last night so she wouldn't have a lot to do today. She'd tossed and turned in an uncomfortable sleeping bag while Lilliana had slept in her playpen. It was still dark when she'd gotten up and thrown on yesterday's jeans and a long-sleeve flannel shirt that had seen better days. She'd yanked her hair into a messy ponytail that no doubt resembled a bird's nest by now. And somehow she'd gotten some of Lilliana's snack on her clothes. She scraped at the orange goo that had dried on her jeans. "You try traveling with a toddler."

"So you're blaming the ketchup and mustard stains on your shirt on Lilliana?"

"No. Those are mine," she admitted, grimacing. She'd eaten one-handed in a fast-food restaurant while trying to keep Lilliana entertained.

"Where is my niece, by the way?"

"She's in the kitchen with Mom, getting her sugar high on."

"It's funny how becoming a grandmother has

made Mom much more easygoing. Remember when we were kids? She didn't let us have cookies before dinner. We had to sneak them and hope she didn't notice."

Jillian laughed as she recalled the many times she'd acted as lookout while Marty, Victor and Grant had raided the cookie jar. "I know. I was scared of getting caught but it was worth the risk."

Marty sprayed the meat with his secret ingredient, closed the grill and then picked up his beer. He gave her a searching look. "So how are you? Really."

She let her smile fall away. She didn't have to pretend to be Happy Hannah with her brother. "Taking it day by day."

Marty nodded, but that gesture held a lot of meaning. In that one movement, he'd let her know that he understood how she felt. And that he was there whenever she needed him. It was good to be back home among people who loved her. People she could depend on. A lump formed in her throat, and it took effort to swallow.

She stood and tugged at her stained shirt. "I guess I'd better go shower and find something decent to wear."

"It wouldn't hurt." He flashed her a smile. "I'll go inside with you. I want to get my chance to spoil my niece."

They stepped inside together. While Marty went

into the kitchen, Jillian climbed the back stairs and headed to her room. She dug out outfits for herself and Lilliana She didn't know what the future held, but it would be easier to face wearing clean clothes. She gave Lilliana a quick bath, dressed her in a cute dress and styled her hair with matching bows before handing her off to Valerie who wanted to show her grandchild off to her friends.

Then it was her turn. After her shower, Jillian dressed in a green cable-knit sweater, black jeans and boots, feeling much better now that she was out of her grungy clothes. Inhaling deeply, she went downstairs and followed the sound of laughter across the backyard.

The party was already in full swing by the time she entered the tent. Heaters had been set up and the space was toasty. Welcoming. Several long tables were set up with a buffet at one end while round tables filled another side, leaving a dance floor in the middle. There was even a DJ. This was a celebration fit for a conquering hero, not a woman coming home to lick her wounds.

She looked around at the people and immediately spotted Erica, her best friend since high school. They hadn't talked much after Jillian had moved away, but when they hugged, the years fell away and they took up where they'd left off.

"I just saw your daughter. Lilliana is gorgeous. And so friendly," Erica said as they dragged chairs from a table to a quiet corner. Jillian knew she would have to make the rounds at some point, but that would have to wait until after she'd caught up with her old friend.

"Thanks. It's so good to see you. I can't believe I let so much time pass without talking to you."

Erica shrugged in her familiar, laid-back way. "I let the same amount of time pass. But we're together now and I'm ready to fill you in on all the Aspen Creek gossip."

Jillian laughed. She knew there would be plenty of funny anecdotes and newsy tidbits, but none of it would be mean-spirited. Erica was too sweet for that. Hopefully none of the stories would involve Miles. She didn't think she could bear to hear about him. She forced him from her mind. What difference would it make if Erica refrained from talking about Miles if Jillian constantly thought of him?

Erica was launching into a story when three of their high school friends joined them.

"So this is where the party people are hanging out," Lauren, a slender woman with a friendly smile, said. Jillian hugged her and then embraced Courtney, Lauren's, fraternal twin. The sisters were part of the close-knit group of friends.

"Erica was just about to get me caught up on all the news."

"You mean the sanitized version. We'll give you

the real dirt later," Courtney said with a mischievous grin.

They laughed. "Did you hear that Theresa retired and moved to Arizona?" Lauren asked.

"No way," Jillian said.

Theresa had been their favorite waitress at the diner. She'd smiled when as preteens they'd plotted ways to get certain boys to notice them, put extra whipped cream on their milkshakes when they hadn't gotten the leads in school plays, and cheered alongside them when they'd achieved a goal.

"Yep. The end of an era," Erica said.

"I hope they gave her a party."

"They did. The whole town showed up. There's a new waitress now, but nobody will ever replace Theresa.

"I'm sorry I missed it."

"Us, too. But you're back now. And you'll be here for everything in the future."

"That's true." She was home now and had no intention of leaving any time soon.

As her friends continued to catch her up on the latest goings on, it began to feel like old times. She'd missed this. Missed them. After a while, Jillian stood. "I guess I need to do the good mother thing and go and find my daughter. And then I need to circulate."

"Speaking of your daughter, there's a playgroup in town that you might want to bring her to. It meets twice a week at the library. I take my nephew there every once in a while," Lauren said.

"That sounds good. I want Lilliana to get into the swing of things as soon as possible."

"I'll text you the information."

Jillian nodded, then headed off to mingle, greeting neighbors and family friends. After making a circuit of the tent, she found Lilliana in the company of Jillian's brothers. Marty was holding her in his arms. Her daughter was frowning and Grant and Victor were trying to get her to smile. Jillian watched in amusement as her brothers played with dolls in an attempt to coax a smile from Lilliana.

"Hey guys," Jillian said. She hugged each of her brothers, taking a moment to savor their strong embraces.

"It's about time you found your way over here," Grant said, holding her at arms' length. "I was beginning to get a complex."

"No way. You know you're my favorite oldest brother." Jillian turned to Victor, "And you're my favorite middle brother."

"And you're our favorite sister."

They all laughed at the old family joke.

Hearing Jillian's voice, Lilliana reached out.

"I guess you're feeling a bit neglected," Jillian said.

"Not hardly," Marty replied. "Lilliana is the star of the show. She's just angry that I won't let her have any of my beer. I might have given her a sip, but I had a feeling you wouldn't like it."

Jillian shook her head as she took Lilliana from Marty. Lilliana reached for the beer and Marty held it away from her, making the baby pout again. "Let's get you some juice of your own."

"Juice?" Lilliana said, clapping her chubby hands.

"Why didn't you say you were thirsty?" Victor asked, grinning. He held out the doll and Lilliana grabbed it and tucked it under her arm. "I would have given you juice."

"Do you want me to get it for you?" Grant asked.

"That's all right. It won't take but a minute." Jillian went into the kitchen where she quickly filled a sippy cup with apple juice and then returned to the party. Dinner was being served and Jillian joined her friends at a table. Valerie took Lilliana, saying she wanted to borrow her for a bit. Jillian knew that was code for give Lilliana whatever she wanted to eat, but it was a party, after all.

"This had to be the best steak I've ever eaten," Courtney said as they finished eating. "I think I might be falling in love with Marty."

"Not again," Lauren said, setting her cutlery on her empty plate and dabbing at her mouth.

Marty had been just the right age for Jillian's friends to have crushes on. When they'd come over, her friends had made a point of running into Marty, dissolving into giggles when he'd speak to them. He was always friendly to them, somewhat amused by the attention. Jillian had never seen the attraction, but then he was her brother. Even so, she'd been glad when her friends had turned their attention to other boys.

"If you weren't a vegetarian, you'd understand," Courtney said.

"I'm not to the point of giving him my heart," Erica added, "but these ribs are the best. A one-or-two-night stand might be in order."

"Please stop," Jillian said, covering her eyes with her hands. "I don't need that image in my head."

Her friends looked at each other and they all laughed. "Only because the DJ is setting up to play," Courtney said.

"Whatever it takes."

The first few bars of music played and they jumped to their feet and headed for the dance floor. The DJ played an endless stream of line dances, so partners weren't necessary. After about twenty minutes or so, Jillian and many of the other women present, had kicked off their heels, a sign that they intended to do some serious partying.

When the DJ announced that he was about to play his last song, there was a chorus of good-natured groaning.

The end of dancing marked the end of the party, and Jillian found herself once more enveloped in hugs. Although she had been happy to see her friends and neighbors, she was also happy when the last guest left. It had been a long day and her bed was calling.

"I'll help with cleanup," she said to her mother as she stepped into the kitchen.

"You'll do no such thing. I know you're tired. Your father put Lilliana in her crib a while ago and she's sleeping soundly, so you don't have to worry about her. Go to bed or put your feet up and read."

"If you're sure," Jillian said, right before she yawned.

"I am." Her mother pulled her into a warm hug. "I can't tell you how happy I am to have you home."

Jillian returned her mother's embrace. "I'm glad to be back. I missed you."

Although she'd had a full day, Jillian was too wired to sleep so she put a coat over her pajamas and sat on the balcony outside her bedroom. Her parents had insisted that their home be as luxurious as the rooms they provided guests at the resort. Of course, there was no room service or housekeeping, but the house was spacious, and Jillian appreciated being able to enjoy the view of the Rockies, something she'd missed while living in Kansas.

As she stared at the mountains in the dark night, she couldn't help but think of Miles and the many nights he'd stood beneath the balcony and called out to her. He could have marched up the front steps and rung the doorbell or called her on the phone. Her parents and his were good friends and Valerie and Henry had adored him. When she'd pointed that out to him, he'd only laughed and said it was more romantic this way. And he'd been right. Her heart had always skipped a beat whenever she heard pebbles click against her sliding doors seconds before he called her name.

Perhaps he'd also been right about ending things. Maybe they had been swept up in the romance of it all and needed a reality check before they took the next step in their relationship. Who knew? Did it matter now? They were over and had been for years. It was water under the bridge.

She hadn't thought of Miles in years so why was he suddenly on her mind? Maybe it was being back home where they'd made so many memories. Whatever the cause, she wasn't going to let it become a habit. Miles Montgomery was out of her life, and she was determined to keep it that way.

Chapter Two

"Jillian is back in town," Miles's mother said as soon as he and Benji stepped into her kitchen for breakfast the next morning Although he and his three-year-old son lived in their own house on the ranch, Michelle babysat Benji while Miles worked. A few times a week he and Benji ate breakfast with his parents. Now Miles was wishing he'd cooked for the two of them today. Of course, there would be no avoiding this conversation, so he might as well get it over with now.

"I know," Miles said, not pointing out that his mother had told him several weeks ago that Jillian would be moving back to Aspen Creek. Michelle had also mentioned that she and his father would be attending her welcome home party last night.

His mother never forgot a thing, so there had to be a reason she was mentioning it yet again.

He set Benji in his booster seat and watched as his son immediately grabbed a strawberry from his plate and shoved it into his mouth as if he hadn't eaten in days.

Michelle raised an eyebrow at Benji's uncharacteristic behavior then glanced at Miles.

Miles sighed. "He didn't want to eat the chicken and rice I cooked for dinner yesterday. But I couldn't get him to tell me what he *wanted* to eat. He rejected all of the options. Finally he ate a few spoonfuls of applesauce and three mozzarella sticks."

Miles had called it a win although he didn't tell his mother that. Now, watching his son shove food into his mouth like a starving man, he was filled with guilt. Perhaps he should have tried harder with dinner yesterday.

His mother put a waffle and a strip of bacon on Benji's plate, then cut the waffle before Miles could. "Aspen Creek is a small town."

"I know that, too," Miles said, filling his own plate and beginning to eat. He glanced at his father, who'd already dug into his breakfast. Edward only shook his head before using his biscuit to scrape up some egg yolk. No help there. Not that Miles expected any. Edward had told Miles and his brothers long ago that there was no sense trying to debate with their mother. They weren't going to win. Better to let her make her point—whatever it was—and get on with things.

"Then I'm suggesting that you and Jillian clear the air. Her parents are our best friends, and we don't want things to become awkward between us because you and Jillian are no longer friends."

"There's no reason why things should become awkward. Our relationship was over years ago and nothing has changed between you."

Saying the words caused an unexpected pang near his heart.

Jillian was the one who'd gotten away. No—Miles frowned. That wasn't entirely accurate. She hadn't *gotten* away. He'd *shoved* her away. True, he'd been younger then—and stupider—but that didn't change the fact that she was no longer a part of his life.

At one time, they'd been as thick as thieves. She'd been more than his best friend and confidant. She'd been his co-conspirator. They'd gotten into so much mischief together during their middle school years—mischief that she'd instigated but that he'd willingly participated in. They'd gone from best friends to boyfriend and girlfriend without missing a beat. He'd often wondered if they'd really been in love or if being in a romantic relationship had been the only way to explain their closeness.

So he'd broken up with her in a disastrous ef-fort to find out. Jillian deserved a man who was one hundred percent in, not one who wasn't sure of his feelings. He and Jillian had been broken up for less than a month when he'd met Rachel who'd been vacationing in Aspen Creek were two of her girlfriends. She'd been looking for fun and he'd been willing to accommodate her. A few weeks later Rachel called, letting him know she was pregnant. They'd married, putting an end to his friendship with Jillian. In hindsight, it was clear that he and Rachel had never been suited. To her, Aspen Creek was a place to visit. To him, it was home. What should have been a holiday fling turned into a joyless marriage that had been doomed from the start.

He knew he shared in the blame with Rachel. She hadn't wanted to get married in the first place. When she'd told him that she was pregnant, she'd been uncertain about everything. He'd convinced her to marry him, have the baby, and move to the ranch.

Rachel had known the marriage was a mistake before he had. She didn't want a life that included getting up before the sun rose and going to bed shortly after it set. She wanted a life filled with fun and adventure. Friends. A life free of smelly cows, barking dogs, acres of nothing. And *him*.

When she'd told Miles how she felt, he'd tried to convince her to stay. And then she'd asked him point blank if he loved her. She must have seen the "no" in his eyes even without him saying the word because she'd admitted that she didn't love him either. Neither of them was happy, but they didn't hate each other. Yet. They both knew that if nothing changed, that would be a possibility. And they didn't want their child to grow up with parents who hated each other.

And so they'd divorced and she'd left, returning to Florida. Needing to rebuild her life, she'd given him primary custody of Benji. She still called Benji weekly and visited him when she could. Even so, for all intents and purposes, Miles was a single father.

"It was one thing when she lived in Kansas City and there was no chance the two of you would see each other" Michelle said, pulling him back to the present. "But now that she's back in town, the two of you are bound to bump into each other. If you don't straighten out things, those interactions will be awkward. And they will naturally cause strain between the rest of us."

"I doubt that. Even if our interactions are tense—not that I expect them to be after all this time—that has nothing to do with your relationship with her parents. Heck, it has nothing to do with *your* relationship with Jillian."

"I know you don't believe that for a minute."

Miles shook his head. No, he didn't. He knew he needed to straighten things out with Jillian. Had known it for a while. But he would prefer to have that conversation at a time in the distant future when he didn't have a choice. And after he'd prepared a speech. He didn't like drama and he didn't see the wisdom in seeking out Jillian and potentially causing a scene. To his way of thinking, it would be better to let Jillian decide when or if they interacted. Aspen Creek was small enough that he was bound to run into her. It wouldn't be hard to figure out if she was avoiding him. If that was what she preferred, then he would go along with it. He wanted the choice to be hers. Given the fact that she hadn't been back in town for twenty-four hours yet, she probably hadn't given it or him a moment's thought.

But on the other hand…it would be good to know one way or the other. And who knew, it was possible Jillian was wondering the same thing about their relationship. It just might be better to approach Jillian instead of leaving everything to chance. The direct approach was better. He'd seek out Jillian and see if she wanted to be friends again.

His heart skipped a beat at the thought, and he glanced around, hoping that his parents hadn't noticed anything. Edward was wiping off a smear of strawberry from Benji's face. However, his mother was looking at him expectantly, her fork suspended in midair, and it took a moment for him to realize that he hadn't responded. "Okay. I'll try to find a time to talk to her before the week is over."

"Why so long?"

"I have work to do. We're repairing some of the barns today."

"We can handle it without you," Edward said.

"Are you sure?"

"Positive. Get this taken care of. Just catch up with us when you're finished. There will still be plenty of work to do."

"Okay. I'll talk to her this morning."

"Good," Michelle said, smiling. "The sooner this is resolved the better."

After breakfast he kissed Benji and reminded him to be good for Grandma. Although there was a preschool in town, Miles preferred to keep Benji nearby during the day. That way, if he had a break in the action, Miles could stop in and spend time with him, something he wouldn't be able to do if Benji was in Aspen Creek. Given that Benji's mother was mostly out of the picture, Miles wanted to be sure Benji knew he was always around. After Rachel left, Michelle had wanted Miles and Benji to move back home so she could help out. Although it had been tempting to take his mother up on her offer, Miles had resisted. Benji was his son, and it was his job to raise him. Miles wasn't above asking for help when he needed it, though, which was why he'd accepted her offer to babysit.

As Miles traveled the familiar route to Jillian's parents' house, he recalled the numerous times he'd driven down this very road to pick up Jillian for a date or to just hang out with her. He smiled as he re-called how she'd open the front door before he was even out of his truck. It had always felt so good to know that she was just as excited to see him as he'd been to see her. But that was before the demise of their relationship. He didn't know how Jillian felt about him now—if she felt anything at all—but he doubted she would eagerly open the door to wel-come him into her house.

The closer he got to the Adamses' house, the more his doubt grew. Maybe showing up out of the blue wasn't the best idea. Perhaps he should have given her a call and tested the water. But he was here now. Truthfully, there would be no easy way to do this. Their first interaction was bound to be uncomfortable no matter when, where or how it occurred. He may as well get it over with now. It would be best to have the conversation in the pri-vacy of her home where they wouldn't be over-heard. The last thing he wanted was to cause a public scene.

He parked, placed his Stetson on his head, and climbed the wide stone stairs to the front porch then inhaled the bracing air before he rang the doorbell. As the bells pealed inside, he mentally reviewed the speech he'd prepared. He suddenly felt jittery and shifted from one foot to the other.

The door swung open, and there she was, as beautiful as ever. His heart lurched, threatening to break free from his chest, and he took a deep breath. She looked so familiar, the intervening years might never have passed. Her brown skin was just as clear, her dark eyes just as intelligent as he remembered. Her high cheekbones and full lips were just as luscious as they'd ever been. She was radiant. Perfection personified.

As he stood there gaping at her, he did notice one major difference. She wasn't smiling. The eyes that had always sparkled with pleasure at seeing him were cold. Frigid even, leaving no doubt about how she felt seeing him standing on her parents' front porch. His mother might be right about most things, but she'd definitely been mistaken about this. There would be no clearing the air with Jillian. Definitely no fresh start. Even so, he didn't want them to be enemies. Aspen Creek was a small town and they would inevitably encounter each other from time to time. He would prefer it if those interactions were civil, if not friendly. And he was here to address the issue.

"Did you want something?" Jillian snapped. Her voice was just as icy and unwelcoming as her expression, and despite knowing that he'd earned this reception, he felt like she could cut him a little bit of slack. They had once been the best of friends.

"I just wanted to welcome you back home." That sounded ridiculous even to him but expressing himself had never been his strong suit. He'd inherited his lack of conversational skills from his father, a man of few words. But Edward had always managed to get his point across while Miles usually fumbled around, trying to find the right words.

She raised an eyebrow but otherwise didn't reply. This silent, distant Jillian was so different from the warm, bubbly Jillian he remembered. It was a shock to his system and he found himself floundering for more words that didn't come. Once she would have filled the silence with happy talk, giving him a chance to relax. But then he'd always been relaxed around Jillian in the past, only needing her to provide cover when he was addressing someone else in a difficult situation. Now it was just the two of them and she wasn't going to jump in and save him.

"Anyway," he added when it became painfully clear that she had no intention of participating in the conversation and the silence stretched uncomfortably, "welcome home."

"If that's all…" she said, stepping back and closing the door.

"Wait." He put his foot inside the doorframe, preventing her from shutting the door in his face.

She blew out a breath and opened the door again. The look she gave him was pure irritation, but at least she was still there. After a few tortuous moments of silence, she spoke. "You're letting the heat out. Did you have more to say? Because believe it or not, I can't read your mind."

He couldn't help but smile at that last comment. When they'd been in high school, she'd sworn that she always knew what he was thinking. That was how in tune they'd been. Until that disastrous dinner.

"Yes. I wanted to apologize."

"For what?"

"I should have handled things better back then."

"No apology is necessary. You made yourself and your feelings perfectly clear. That's all that was required. Now, if there's nothing more, I have things to do."

Once more she started to close the door and he grabbed it. Her eyes widened in surprise. This behavior was so uncharacteristic of him.

"Uh, actually there is more."

She blew out a breath. "What?"

He searched his mind for the right thing to say, but he was distracted by her beauty. Even after all this time, there was something about Jillian that reached him in a way that no other woman had. It pained him to think that their connection had been irrevocably broken.

"I hope that we can become friends again."

She huffed a laugh, but it didn't hold even the slightest bit of humor. "You're serious?"

Although his words were as surprising to him as they appeared to be to her, he realized that he actually meant what he said. He wanted her back in his life. "Yes."

"Never in this lifetime, Miles. And if there is a next lifetime, not in that one either." She grabbed the door and narrowed her eyes as she stared daggers at him. "Now move your foot or lose it."

He moved his foot seconds before the door slammed shut, leaving his standing in the falling snow. He heard the lock engage and knew that she was locking him out of her life just as firmly.

Jillian leaned against the front door, her heart pounding. She didn't dare move until she heard the engine of Miles's pickup truck rumble as he drove down the driveway. Even so, she stood stock-still until she could no longer hear the sound. Only then did she trust her wobbly legs to carry her to the living room where she slumped onto the sofa.

Whew. She knew she would eventually have to face Miles, but she didn't expect to see him so soon. And she certainly didn't expect him to just ring her doorbell with no advance warning like that. Would a week's reprieve be too much to ask? Thank goodness Lilliana was napping and her parents were at work, so she didn't need to pretend that everything was wonderful. She'd excelled at pretending her marriage was fine, but she wasn't skillful enough to act as if seeing Miles hadn't knocked her for a loop.

The memories of times she'd spent with Miles began to bombard her and she shoved them away. She wasn't going to go skipping down memory lane as if everything had been rosy between them. She might have believed that at the time, but she'd been wrong. She'd been thinking about marriage and a life together, and he'd been looking for a way out so he could date any woman who caught his eye. And there had been a lot of them dancing in and out of his life. Though he'd claimed he hadn't wanted a commitment, he'd soon married one of those women and had a child with her. Clearly, Miles hadn't been opposed to marriage. He just hadn't wanted to marry her. Even after all this time, that reality still stung with the pain of rejection.

The depth of her anger had come as a surprise. Just last night she'd thought he might have been right to end things between them. But that had been the rational part of her entertaining an abstract idea. Coming face-to-face with him had brought back actual anger and devastation that had erupted to the surface before she could control it. Maybe she wasn't as over the past as she wanted to believe.

Lilliana called out to her from the bedroom, pulling Jillian from her reverie. And just in time. She couldn't afford to relive the past. Thinking about what might have been didn't change a thing. All it did was make her feel bad and wonder what she'd done to send him running away from her and into the arms of another woman. That wasn't productive and she wasn't going to travel down that miserable path ever again.

Lilliana called out again and Jillian hurried up the stairs to her daughter. Lilliana was standing in her crib, shaking the side with one hand, clenching her favorite teddy bear in the other. When she spotted Jillian, Lilliana gave a cheery grin. "Mama."

"Yep. Mama's here." Jillian picked up Lilliana and held her tight against her chest. This was all the love she needed in the world. Her romantic relationships might have flamed out spectacularly, but there was nothing quite like her daughter's love.

"Let's change that wet diaper and get you a snack."

"Mack," Lilliana said, clapping her hands. She had a limited vocabulary and only now was beginning to speak in the occasional two-word sentence, but she understood quite a few words. Snack was one of her favorites.

After a quick diaper change, Jillian carried her daughter down to the kitchen where she gave her sliced apples, cheese and a cup of milk. While her daughter ate, Jillian checked her phone, rereading the text Lauren had sent her about the playgroup. Lilliana was a social butterfly who loved being around other children, so she should enjoy playgroup immensely.

Being a part of a group would do Jillian good, too. She'd never been the type to spend a lot of time alone, preferring to get together with friends. She thrived on interacting with others. Socializing was more necessary now when it would be so easy to mope around, thinking about her failed marriage and her disastrous relationship with Miles. She needed to get back into the swing of things sooner rather than later, and start a routine that included friends her age.

Having that to look forward to made unpacking the rest of their belongings go more quickly. When she'd folded the last moving box, she was tired, but filled with anticipation for the next day's adventure.

The next morning, Jillian drove to Aspen Creek and, despite wanting to take a look around town, she went directly to the public library where the playgroup met. The three-story redbrick building fit in perfectly on the quaint downtown street. She and Lilliana had arrived fifteen minutes early so that Jillian could complete the necessary paperwork, meet the group leader and take a look around. When she'd lived here, Jillian hadn't spent much time in the library, preferring to purchase her books at the local bookstore, so when she stepped inside, she was pleasantly surprised.

The library was more than a place to borrow books and do research for term papers. It also functioned as the Aspen Creek community center. Bright posters and flyers advertised movie night for middle-grade kids, craft evenings for primary grades and science projects for high school kids. There were computer classes for adults and other events planned. She realized she'd cheated herself out of a valuable resource by not coming here when she was younger.

Jillian set Lilliana on the floor beside her, and, holding hands, they walked to the curved front desk. The woman working there glanced up and smiled. "Good morning."

"Hi. I'm Jillian Adams and this is my daughter, Lilliana. I spoke with someone about the playgroup."

"That someone would be me. Welcome. I'm Veronica Kendricks. I'm the children's librarian and I run the group. Let's take a look around," she said, coming from behind the desk. She knelt down in front of Lilliana. "Aren't you a cutie?"

Veronica tapped Lilliana on the nose, earning a wide smile in return. "Hi."

"Hi," Lilliana replied.

"Let's get this tour started," Veronica said, leading them down a hallway to the right. The building was much bigger than it appeared on the outside. After pointing out the bathrooms, Veronica showed them two large meeting rooms. One was filled with tables and had inspirational posters hanging on the walls. "We use these rooms for everything from business meetings to study halls for teens, to art classes."

"Wow. You really do a lot here," Jillian said.

"Absolutely. We're a small town, but our citizens have the same needs and desires as people in big cities, so we do all we can to meet those needs."

"I actually grew up in Aspen Creek, but sadly didn't take advantage of the library back then."

Veronica smiled. "You're here now, that's what matters. And you're getting your daughter off on the right track." Veronica led them to the stairs. Jillian picked up Lilliana and followed Veronica to the second floor. It was a large, open, multipurpose space. Computers lined one wall, most of which were in use. There were several shelves filled with books. The children's section was on the far side of the room. Large floor-to-ceiling windows illuminated the area. Colorful pillows and stuffed animals were arranged around child-size tables and chairs. A woman was sitting on the rug holding a toddler on her lap and reading softly from a children's book.

"This is very nice," Jillian said.

"I'm glad you think so," Veronica said. "I try to make the space appealing, so our little ones develop a love of reading. I want the library to be a place they associate with happiness and a good time. I don't want kids to grow up thinking reading is a chore or some sort of punishment."

Jillian nodded.

Veronica blew out a breath. "Sorry. I didn't mean to get on a rant. Children's literacy is just so important to me."

"Don't worry about it. You weren't ranting. You're passionate. There's nothing wrong with that."

They quickly finished the tour and then went to the meeting room that had been set up for the playgroup. The room was alive with activity as moms bustled about, helping their kids remove their coats and boots. Other children were grouped around several bins, pulling out toys willy-nilly. Two boys were standing near the ladder of a small indoor slide while another kid took his turn. Several little girls were playing in a mini kitchen while women, who Jillian assumed were the little girls' mothers, clustered nearby, chatting while they kept a watchful eye on the children.

Jillian had hoped to see a familiar face, but the other women were at least five or more years older than she was and their lives hadn't intersected at any point.

"What do you want to play with?" Jillian asked Lilliana. Without the slightest bit of hesitation, Lilliana toddled over to building blocks that had been set up in the middle of the room and plopped down on the rug. Within seconds, she was placing the blocks on top of each other, making a tower and humming happily to herself. Jillian sat beside her, counting aloud as Lilliana added blocks.

After she'd piled up six blocks, the tower came crashing to the floor.

"Uh-oh," a little boy of about three said as he

raced over. He was still wearing his coat, but that didn't stop him. "I'll help."

Before Jillian could say a word, the boy had dropped onto the floor beside Lilliana. He picked up two blocks and offered one to Lilliana. She looked at him for a brief moment as if deciding how she felt about this new kid joining her. Then she smiled and took the block from him.

A moment later a shadow fell over the trio and Jillian looked up, expecting to see the little boy's mother. Instead she was staring directly into Miles's face. He smiled and, before she could react, sat beside her on the rug. His denim-clad knee brushed against hers and she felt the slightest shiver, which she ignored. She wasn't going to allow any latent attraction to Miles to spring to life and lead her on the path to heartache and disappointment. He might still be as attractive as he'd been years ago, even more so if she was being honest, but that was neither here nor there. She couldn't be taken in by his gorgeous brown skin, handsome face, warm eyes and brilliant smile. Not when she knew that he lacked the depth of personality to match his attractive appearance.

"Hi, Jillian. I didn't expect to see you here today." His voice was warm and tinged with surprise. And if she was accurate, delight.

"I could say the same thing about you." Of course,

she wasn't as happy about his presence as he appeared to be about hers.

"Benji and I are members of the playgroup, aren't we, buddy?" Miles helped his son take off his coat and then looked at Jillian as he removed his own cowboy hat. "The blocks are his favorite toy, with the trucks coming in a close second. Ordinarily if someone else is playing with the blocks, he just grabs a truck, so I'm surprised that he came over here to play with your daughter."

Lilliana babbled a few garbled words and then held out her hand to Benji. He smiled and handed her another block. Lilliana beamed at Benji and then added the block to the tower. Miles shook his head. "Or maybe I'm not surprised."

"What does that mean?"

"Your little girl is a cutie. And she seems sweet as pie. Benji didn't stand a chance of resisting her."

"Lilliana has always been friendly. She skipped the shy phase and has never met a kid she didn't like," Jillian said affectionately. "Of course, she's new to the terrible twos, so who knows what they'll bring."

Jillian found herself smiling and quickly bit it back. She didn't want Miles to think they were going to become friends. In fact, if she could find a way to take her daughter to another part of the room without making a scene, she would. But since

Lilliana was enjoying herself, Jillian turned away from Miles and looked back at the children.

"Good job," Benji said, clapping his hands as he set a block on the ever-growing tower. He looked like a miniature version of Miles from his rich brown skin to his dimpled cheeks.

"Goo bob," Lilliana echoed, clapping her hands, too.

"Your tower is getting so tall," Jillian said. "Maybe you should stand up so you can add more blocks."

"Okay," Benji said and then stood.

Lilliana echoed Benji and then scrambled to her feet, copying his movements, too. While the kids gathered more blocks, Miles straightened the tower, keeping it from tumbling to the floor. One of the blocks came free and started to fall so Jillian reached out to grab it. She and Miles moved at the same time and their hands brushed. A slight frisson of excitement skittered down her spine at the contact and she yanked her hand away. If Miles noticed her reaction, he had the good sense not to mention it. Instead, he straightened the tower and moved back.

The children stacked the blocks for a few more minutes until the tower was over Benji's head and they could no longer add more blocks. Benji and Lilliana stood back and admired their work for a moment, grinning from ear to ear. Then, without warning, they each attacked the tower, knocking it over.

"Fall down," Lilliana said, chortling loudly.

"Yep," Benji agreed, stooping over to pick up the blocks.

"How about we find something else to play with?" Jillian asked Lilliana as she pulled her daughter into her arms for a quick hug. This break in the action was the perfect time to get away from Miles without being too obvious.

"'Kay," Lilliana agreed.

"We'll see you later, Benji," Jillian said to the little boy. She ignored Miles altogether as she steered Lilliana across the room to a table where crayons and construction paper were scattered. Another little girl was sitting there and she smiled at Lilliana before trading in her green crayon for a red one and scribbling happily on her paper.

Lilliana sat down and Jillian set a piece of paper in front of her, stepped back and watched as her daughter grabbed a purple crayon and began to draw. After a moment, she went to stand beside another woman who was watching the children play.

"I'm Traci," she said with a friendly smile. "That's my daughter Marissa at the table with your daughter."

Jillian smiled and introduced herself.

"Are you new to town?" Traci asked, her eyes brimming with curiosity.

"I was raised here, but I moved away three years ago. I recently got divorced and moved back in with my parents. A friend told me about the group, and I decided to bring Lilliana and check it out."

"Sounds like you moved away right before my family and I moved to town. We're a good group. The kids are nice and for the most part well-behaved, and the adults are friendly. You'll fit right in."

"Thanks."

They chatted about Aspen Creek and changes that had occurred while Jillian had been gone. There hadn't been very many. It was still a tourist town with a steady influx of people who came to enjoy nature before returning to their regularly scheduled lives. A few new families had moved in, but everything still felt the same. Although Jillian was one to go with the flow, she was glad for the familiarity. There had been enough change and upheaval in her life recently. Steadiness was a good thing. She would even welcome a bit of redundancy. Anything that would mean her life was settling down and becoming happily predictable.

Without her permission, her eyes strayed to where Miles stood. She watched as he rolled a ball back and forth with his son and another little boy. He was the only father in the group of fifteen or so moms, and Jillian couldn't help but wonder where his wife was. Not that she would ask him or anyone else.

After he'd dumped her so unceremoniously, she'd made her friends and family swear that they would never mention him or his wife to her. Anything to do with Miles was off-limits. They'd kept that promise, so she knew nothing about him or his life over the past few years. A part of her wished that someone had mentioned that Miles and his son attended the playgroup so she would have been forewarned. But Jillian knew she couldn't have it both ways. Besides, if she had known that Miles's son was part of the group, she might not have come. That would have been unfair to Lilliana. Jillian and her family might adore her and give her plenty of attention, but Lilliana needed to be around other children.

The other mothers seemed to have accepted Miles as one of the group. A mother had joined them on the floor and the quartet played with the ball. Miles and the other woman appeared cozy, and Jillian wondered whether his wife would approve. She forced that thought away. Miles's relationship with his wife—or anyone else—was none of her concern. In fact, nothing Miles did was her business.

"We're about to transition into story time," Traci said, pulling Jillian's attention away from Miles and back to the present where it belonged. "Veronica leads the kids in cleanup, and then they gather on the rug and sing songs, and she reads a couple of books. The adults go to the other room and have coffee."

Jillian followed the other women as they began heading into the adjoining meeting room. She tried not to notice that Miles was walking beside the same woman he'd been with before, talking quietly with her. Incredibly, she felt a twinge of jealousy, which was ridiculous. Miles had shown her long ago that she wasn't the woman for him. His heart would never belong to her.

"Do you know Miles?" Traci asked as she filled a cup with coffee and then added sugar.

"Yes." Jillian didn't elaborate, hoping the other woman would take the hint that Jillian didn't want to talk about Miles.

"He's a good guy. All the moms adore him. And Benji is a sweet little boy. He usually plays by himself, so I was surprised to see him with your little girl."

"Lilliana has that effect on everyone. She's a people magnet and can pull the shyest child out of his shell. Unless she's sleepy. Then she doesn't want to be bothered."

They laughed together. Miles and the other woman approached the table, so Jillian took her cup and started to move away.

"Have you met Lydia?" Miles asked, stopping her

mid-escape. It would be rude to pretend she hadn't heard him.

"No," Jillian replied, turning her attention to the woman by Miles's side. "I'm Jillian."

"It's nice to meet you," Lydia said, smiling. "Welcome. I hope you and your daughter enjoy our playgroup."

"I'm sure we will."

Lydia and Traci excused themselves and then went to join another group of moms, leaving Jillian alone with Miles. Out of nowhere, the hurt and anger she'd felt when he'd dumped her came back with full force and she did her best to squelch it. The last thing she wanted to do was reveal her deep, lingering emotions.

"What do you think of the group?"

"I feel like everyone here has asked me some variation of that question." Three other mothers had introduced themselves to her while she'd been talking to Traci and had asked the same thing.

He chuckled, unbothered by her cranky response. "That's because we're a close-knit bunch. We want everyone who attends to know that they're welcome."

"Are you the only dad who comes?"

He nodded. "For the most part. Every once in a while another dad or two will come, but it's generally just me. I don't mind, though."

"So why doesn't your wife come?" Jillian asked.

Instantly she wanted to bite her tongue, but it was too late to recall the words. She'd indicated to Miles that she was interested in his life, something that he didn't need to know.

"I'm divorced. I have primary custody of Benji."

"Really? Why is that?" The second the question was out of her mouth, she wanted to call it back. She waved a hand in the air as if erasing her words. "Forget I said that. It's none of my business."

"And you don't want to give me the impression that you care about me." He sounded smug, a trait that didn't fit in with the memory of the Miles she'd grown up with. Clearly she didn't know him as well as she'd thought she had. She compressed her lips to keep from replying.

"What's that old saying? *A nice place to visit but I wouldn't want to live there?* Living on a ranch in the middle of nowhere with nothing but cows for company didn't suit her. Rachel was a city girl. So she went back where she felt happiest. I agreed with her decision."

Jillian knew there had to be more to the story, but she didn't pry. Although Miles had spoken matter-of-factly, Jillian knew him too well to be fooled. He'd been hurt. And disappointed. She blinked. Wait a minute. No way she was going to pity him.

This was what he'd had coming. Then she thought about his sweet little boy. How he must miss his mother. He deserved to have her in his life just as Lilliana deserved to have her father in her life. The children were innocent; voiceless in the decisions that affected their lives. Her heart ached just as much for Benji as it did for her own little girl.

Despite feeling sympathy for his son, Jillian couldn't think of anything to say that wouldn't be petty. Silence was the best and kindest response in this situation.

"I just thought you should know," he said.

"Why?" Surely he didn't think she was looking for a second chance.

That seemed to flummox him and he stood with his mouth gaping open for a moment. Finally he spoke again. "I don't know. I just feel like it's fair. I know you're divorced and that you're starting over with your little girl. It seems a bit…unfair that I know more about your life than you know about mine."

"Unfair? Since when is life fair? And when have you started caring about my feelings or being fair to me?"

Chapter Three

Miles paused at Jillian's furious words. They felt like a slap in the face. He knew she believed what she was saying, which made it worse. "I *was* trying to be fair to you, Jillian."

"When? When you led me on, making me think you and I had a future? Was that you being fair to me?" Her voice was quiet, so it didn't carry, but he didn't miss the emotion there. Given how worked up she was becoming, there was the possibility that the conversation could become heated and attract attention, something he didn't want. There'd been more than enough gossip about him around town when Rachel left. Benji had been too young to understand what was happening, but he was older now and that might not still be the case.

"Let's step outside on the patio where we can have a bit more privacy," he said. He took her arm to steer her out the French doors at the far side of the room. She stepped away, but not before he felt a jolt of electricity at the contact. Just what he didn't need. Perhaps the cold weather would cool him off.

At five feet nine, she was seven inches shorter than his own six foot four, but she was angry, and her strides easily matched his.

When they were standing outside, she turned to glare at him, her arms folded over her chest. She was glorious. Her dark brown eyes flashed with anger, but it didn't detract from her beauty. With light brown skin, high cheekbones and full lips, she had always been the most beautiful girl in Aspen Creek. The years had only made her more so.

"Well? What else did you want to say?" she asked. The wind gusted, blowing her thick black curls into her face. She shivered and tossed her head, sending her hair cascading over her shoulder. Snow flurries were falling, but she didn't seem to notice.

"I just wanted you to know my marital status. It's hard being in the dark. I don't want that for you and me so if there's something you want to know, feel free to ask."

"There's absolutely nothing I want to know about your life. To be honest, I couldn't care less about your marital status or anything else. Do you expect me to feel bad because you got dumped by your wife? I don't. Do I want your pity because things didn't work out between me and Lilliana's father? Not even a little bit."

He rubbed his hand over his jaw. Maybe talking to Jillian was a bad idea. Since they were going to see each other at playgroup, he didn't want things to be tense between them. He'd wanted to clear the air, but it looked like he'd only made matters worse. They weren't going to be friends again. Which was too bad because she was the best friend he'd ever had. "I wasn't looking for pity. I just thought you should know."

"Well, now I know. And now you know I don't care."

He nodded. That should have been enough, but it wasn't. "I just don't want things to be unpleasant between us."

She sighed and gave him a look he couldn't decipher. "Miles, there is no us. Maybe there never was."

Before he could tell her how wrong she was, she turned and walked away, leaving him alone on the patio. He replayed the conversation in his mind, trying to figure out what he could have said that would have made things go more smoothly, but he came up empty. Given their history, he shouldn't be surprised by how poorly things had gone. But he was.

Over the past two years, he'd been so busy being a single dad that he hadn't given much thought to his personal life. Raising a son on his own, especially one whose mother lived so far away, was hard and didn't leave time for romantic relationships. Not that he wanted to bring a woman into his life. He and Benji were a crew of two. They didn't need anyone else. They'd been hurt when Rachel left, and neither of their hearts needed to be subjected to the possibility of yet more pain if a relationship didn't work out. Even so, he would be lying to himself if he didn't admit that there had been times when he'd thought about Jillian. Times when he'd wondered how his life would have turned out if he hadn't ended things with her.

He checked his watch. He had to go back inside for the last few minutes of playgroup. Besides, he was getting cold. Benji needed him, so Miles couldn't afford to get sick. He joined the women, making sure to keep his distance from Jillian. That was easy, since she seemed to sense when he'd entered the room and crossed to the far side.

Miles tried to convince himself that he wasn't disappointed, but he knew he was deceiving himself. He'd missed Jillian after their friendship had ended. Her absence had created a hole in his life that he hadn't been able to fill. It would have been wrong to contact her while they were married to other people and he hadn't once tried. But they were both single now. Surely they could find a way to rebuild their friendship. He squashed the notion before it could take root. He had no idea what had happened in Jillian's marriage. Had she been the one who'd wanted the divorce? Or had her husband decided that he wanted out? If so, was Jillian still in love with the other man? Was she hoping that, if given enough time, he would come back into her life? And was he actually gone? Miles had no idea if she and her ex-husband shared custody of Lilliana. Perhaps they were co-parenting and would spend time doing family activities that Rachel's distance made impossible for them.

And why on earth was he spending so much time thinking about Jillian's life? She'd made it perfectly clear that what she and Miles had shared in the past was over, leaving no seeds that could blossom into friendship again.

The kids began singing the goodbye song and Miles pulled his attention back to the present, joining the rest of the parents in singing. The last strains of the song signaled that playgroup had come to an end and the children scattered, racing to their parents. Benji was usually one of the first kids to break the circle, so Miles was surprised to see that his son hadn't come to join him but rather was holding hands with Lilliana and standing in front of Jillian.

He was looking up at her, talking as if they were old friends, something that was completely out of character. Benji was a quiet child who generally kept to himself, which was one of the reasons Miles had decided to enroll him in this playgroup. It was a way for Benji to be around other children while feeling safe in the knowledge that his father was nearby. Miles hoped that Benji would eventually become comfortable enough to attend preschool when he turned four. This could be a sign that Benji was making progress.

Or maybe it was a sign that Jillian's daughter had captivated Benji in the same way that a younger Jillian had captivated a younger Miles. There was something about Jillian that had always drawn him, though he had yet to determine what it was. It was too easy to call it love. He'd felt this intense pull when they'd been kids and he hadn't held even a sliver of romantic interest in her. Heck, he hadn't even known what love was at that age. He'd just always been enchanted by her. And Benji seemed to be just as awestruck by Lilliana as Miles had always been with Jillian.

Miles stepped around a couple of kids as he crossed the room. As he neared the small group he heard Benji chattering on, telling Jillian about playing a game with Lilliana, who was looking at him with adoration. Apparently Lilliana was just as enamored with Benji as he was with her. Jillian smiled and then replied to Benji. He could hear her voice but was unable to make out her words. Whatever she'd said must have been funny because Benji laughed. After a second, Lilliana laughed, too.

The happiness that radiated from his son made Miles smile. Jillian might not like *him*, but she was being kind to his son. More than kind, she was being open and welcoming. Miles couldn't ask for more than that.

Jillian looked up. When she caught Miles staring at her, her smile faded and the air around her cooled. The moment was over.

"You dad is here, Benji."

Benji grinned up at him and the disappointment that had threatened at Jillian's chilliness faded. His relationship with Jillian might have died a miserable death years ago, but he wouldn't trade his son for anything. Including Jillian's friendship. He just wished there was a way to have both.

"Ready to go, buddy?" Miles asked.

"Yep. Bye, Lily."

"Bye-bye, bye, bye, Enji," Lilliana said. She dropped his hand and then wrapped her chubby arms around his middle. Benji looked startled by the unexpected gesture. Then he grinned and returned the toddler's hug.

"Bye, Jilly," Benji said.

"Bye, Benji. See you later."

Miles took Benji's hand at the same time that Jillian took Lilliana's, and they got the children dressed in their outerwear and left the library. Since they were walking in the same direction, they ended up walking together. Benji talked easily to Lilliana, who babbled indecipherable words in response. They'd parked on opposite ends of the parking lot, so when they reached the sidewalk, the kids repeated the goodbyes before they all parted.

Once Benji was buckled into his booster seat, Miles put all thoughts of Jillian and her sweet daughter out of his mind as he drove to the ranch. Taking Benji to playgroup wreaked havoc on his schedule, and he often had to skip lunch to catch up, but his son was worth it. Miles's mother had offered to take Benji to playgroup, but Miles had turned her down. Benji was his responsibility. Besides, he liked having this special time with his son.

They reached the main house and went inside where his mother awaited. After he got his son settled with his toy horses in the family room, he turned to his mother, who was stirring a pot on the stove. He didn't know what she was cooking but it smelled delicious.

"I'll be back to pick him up by five thirty."

"You're welcome to join us for dinner," his mother said as always. Miles knew Michelle meant well, but he wouldn't take her up on the offer. She was already doing more than any grandmother should. He didn't want to burden her more. Besides, he and Benji were creating their own family unit.

"Thanks, but I'll pass. I have dinner planned for us. It won't be as good as yours, but it'll do the trick."

His mother patted his cheek. "You're a good dad. I'm proud of you. But you don't have to do it all alone. And you're entitled to have a life of your own. Everything doesn't need to revolve around Benji."

"I know that." Miles still harbored hope that Rachel would want to become a bigger part of Benji's life. Until that happened he needed to do more than other parents.

"And it would do him good if you met a nice girl and settled down again. He could use a loving stepmother."

This was a first. Michelle knew he'd been hurt when Rachel left and that he wasn't interested in having a relationship. His mother hadn't argued. In fact, she'd agreed that he needed to put Benji first. But that was before Jillian moved back to town. Was Jillian the reason his mother was singing a different tune? She'd go back to the old song if she knew how angry Jillian was. Not that he'd mention it. He didn't want to damage his mother's opinion of Jillian.

Michelle had always liked Jillian. Although she had kept her own counsel when he and Jillian had broken up, he knew she'd been disappointed. Miles had always believed Michelle had held out hope that they would reconcile. But that was before Rachel had gotten pregnant and they'd gotten married.

But he was divorced now, and Jillian was back in town. He could practically see the wheels in his mother's head spinning. She was going to be sorely disappointed to discover that there was no chance that he and Jillian would get back together. If she had seen the frigid look in Jillian's eyes, she would know that even being friends was outside the realm of possibility. Time had definitely changed them from the best of friends into two distant strangers. Heck, if Jillian's attitude was anything to go by, they were enemies.

"I'll think about it," he said, hoping to put an end to the conversation.

She laughed. "No, you won't, but thanks for saying that."

"I will think about it. But the truth is, *think* is all that I have time to do. Between raising Benji and ranching, my schedule is pretty full. And let's face it, being a rancher's wife isn't for everyone. It certainly wasn't right for Rachel."

"I know. The two of you were mismatched from the beginning. She liked city living and everything that a city has to offer. And there's nothing wrong with that. You need someone who likes small-town life."

"Are you suggesting that I start dating one of the single women in town? I suppose I could ask Veronica out on a date. Benji likes her."

Michelle shot him a dirty look and he laughed. It was clear who Michelle had in mind.

He kissed his mother's cheek. "I've got to go. See you later."

Once he was outside, he took a deep breath then slowly blew it out. The familiar scent of the ranch – fresh air mingled with hay with just a touch of pine – always soothed him. No matter where he went in the world, nothing compared to being on the ranch where he'd been raised. Which was why he understood Rachel's desire to return to a place where she felt most comfortable. He only wished that she felt comfortable being a mother to her child.

Although he'd tried to pretend that everything was okay with his mother, he couldn't fool himself. After Rachel left, Miles had worked hard to ensure that he and Benji were fine on their own. He might not have been in love with Rachel, but she'd been his wife. He'd thought they'd be together until death parted them. Although he knew it was for the best, he'd been disappointed when it hadn't worked out that way.

But then Miles had seen Jillian. She was even more beautiful than she'd been years ago. And just as magnetic. He might have held out hope for their friendship if she hadn't been so chilly to him. She was friendly by nature and hadn't been able to hold a grudge for long, so the fact that she was still so angry at him didn't bode well for a future relationship. Perhaps it was time he accepted that reality.

"Are you just going to stand there posing, or are you going to get to work?"

Miles turned at the sound of his brother's amused voice. Isaac was a year younger than Miles and the comedian of the family. He never took anything too seriously. But then, as the youngest child, he'd never had the same responsibilities as Miles and Nathan, their oldest brother. All three brothers got along well, which made the workday go that much more smoothly. Miles knew that he could always depend on his brothers to have his back.

Miles laughed and adjusted his black cowboy hat. "You mean this isn't the photo shoot?"

"You wish."

They saddled their horses, and then headed out, talking as they rode together to check the fence. There were two hundred acres of fencing surrounding the fields, so odds were they would need to repair a bit of it.

"So, I hear Jillian's divorced and back in town," Isaac said after a few minutes.

"You heard right."

"Are the two of you getting back together? Or are you just friends?"

"I can definitely say we're not getting back together. And if by just friends you mean her eyes shooting daggers at me and barely managing to be polite, then yes. We're best pals."

"I don't understand why she's upset. Especially

after all this time. You broke up. It happens. You'd been together since you were in diapers. What man wouldn't want to see what else was out there? I know I would. Heck, the thought of being with the same woman more than a week makes me break out in hives."

"You're definitely allergic to commitment."

"You got that right." Isaac faked a sneeze to emphasize the point and then laughed. "And she got married so she couldn't have been too broken up."

"Who knows? None of our friends who were couples in high school are still together but they still manage to be civil to each other. But she must have her reasons. I'll just accept them and move on."

"You're a better man than I. Don't get me wrong, I always liked Jillian. But I would tell her where to get off."

"That's not necessary. Things will work out or they won't. I've got Benji to worry about, and nothing matters more to me than him, so I can't sweat it."

Even as he heard himself say the words, Miles wished that they would work out. Because seeing Jillian again had made him realize just how much he'd missed her friendship.

Chapter Four

·"How was playgroup?" Valerie asked as soon as Jillian stepped into the house.

"Fine. Miles was there with his son." And why was that the first thing out of her mouth? Couldn't she talk about anyone besides Miles Montgomery?

"Benji is a sweet boy."

"Why didn't you warn me he'd be there?"

"How was I supposed to know he would be? Besides, you're the one who insisted that you never wanted to hear Miles's name again."

Jillian sighed. She had been adamant. Her parents had tried mentioning him once or twice about a year ago and Jillian had blown a gasket. She'd even threatened to never speak to them again if they did. Now she wondered if she'd overreacted a bit. The answer wasn't long in coming. She had gone way over the line.

"You're right. I just wasn't expecting to see him there."

"And if you would have known, would you have deprived Lilliana of the opportunity to make new friends?"

"Of course not."

"Then it really doesn't matter, does it?"

"I suppose not." Jillian sighed. She was being irrational, and she knew it. It was just that seeing Miles two days in a row had knocked her off-kilter. She'd hoped to have time to regain her equilibrium before a second encounter. "Lilliana had a blast."

"So you'll be going back?"

"Of course." She wasn't going to allow Miles to make her hole up in this house out of fear of seeing him again. She'd never give him that much control of her life. "Lilliana needs friends in her life."

"I agree. She's definitely a people person. As are you."

"I am. Now that I'm getting her involved and establishing a routine, I need to do the same for myself."

"Meaning?"

"I want to go back to work."

"Now?"

"Yes. I need to pull my weight around here."

"You haven't even been home a week. Give yourself and Lilliana time to settle in before you start making big changes."

"Lilliana is used to me going to work. I had a full-time job when I lived in Kansas. She went to day care and did quite well. She was the most popular kid there. She thrives on activity and loves being around other kids. She'd be bored out of her head with just adults for company all day, every day."

"Like mother like daughter, I suppose."

"And grandmother."

Valerie nodded. She couldn't claim that Jillian had gotten her personality from her father. Henry was quiet and introspective, just as comfortable reading a book in front of a fire or skiing the slopes alone as he was in a crowded room. Truth be told, he often seemed to prefer his own company. Valerie and Henry were as opposite as any two people could be, but they'd made their relationship work for close to four decades. They loved each other fiercely, but it was more than that. They respected each other's differences. Most importantly, they genuinely liked each other and had fun together.

Her parents had always been her role models and inspiration for the marriage she wanted to have. Jillian had always known that she and Miles had different personalities, but she'd believed they could make a relationship work just as her parents had. Jillian and Miles had been friends forever and things had always clicked between them. She'd believed their relationship was destined to be as successful as her parents'. She couldn't have been more wrong.

Why was she *still* thinking about him? Hadn't she decided not to waste any more time doing that? Their time had come and gone and there was no place for him in her life now. Or her thoughts.

"I suppose you want to come to work at the resort."

"Yes. I loved working there." There was something about working at the family business that just felt right. She liked doing her part to make the resort better for visitors and more successful for her family.

Aspen Creek Resort was family-owned, but it was comparable to the corporate resorts, providing every amenity the other resorts provided and some they didn't. In addition to providing outdoor sports in every season, they had a full service spa. They hosted weddings on the mountain from spring through the early fall. At that time of year, the mountains were filled with beautiful wildflowers and made a perfect backdrop for wedding photos. And the resort had hot springs that were popular all year long.

The town of Aspen Creek also had very popular seasonal festivals that drew in even more vacationers. In the summer, there were balloon rides and street fairs where local restaurant owners showcased their fare. There were scavenger hunts, dances and concerts at the park where local bands performed in front of enthusiastic crowds. Jillian looked forward to attending some of those events in the future and sharing those experiences with her daughter. She knew Lilliana wouldn't appreciate all of the offerings, but she would enjoy the face painting and games geared for preschoolers.

"There are a couple of openings. It really depends on you and how many hours you want to put in. Do you want to work in the shop selling gear, or do you want to handle the front desk? Or would you rather schedule special events?"

"I'll take special events."

"I figured you would. When should I add you to the schedule?"

"Maybe two weeks from now. That'll give me and Lilliana a chance to get into a groove."

"Okay. And if you need more time, you know I'll give it to you."

"That's because you're the world's best mom."

"And don't you forget it." Valerie paused. "This may not be exactly what you're thinking of since it's not quite a special event, but the Chamber of Commerce meets monthly."

Jillian laughed. "And you want me to go?"

"Yes. You know how I hate those things."

"Done. Do I have authority to commit the resort to fundraisers."

"Yes. Use your best judgment."

"Then consider me the resort's representative."

"That's because you're the world's best daughter."

"And don't you forget it."

Jillian made Lilliana's favorite lunch of grilled cheese and tomato soup, and as they ate together, Lilliana chatted happily. Jillian didn't understand everything her daughter said, but she nodded along anyway.

Lilliana did repeat one name often –'Enji – throughout the day. It was clear Miles's son had made a big impact on Lilliana. Evidently Benji, and by extension, Miles, were going to be a part of Jillian's life. Whether or not she liked it.

After she put Lilliana to bed, Jillian began to feel restless. She felt the call of the mountains, so she went outside and sat by the firepit. The evening was cold, but her jacket kept her warm. It was dark and quiet. Soothing. The full moon and countless stars illuminated the sky. She loved this time of night.

Long ago, this had been the time she and Miles had spent together. He'd finish his work on the ranch and she'd finish her duties at the resort, and they'd have the rest of the night to themselves. In the winter they'd meet up and either skate or ski. In the spring and summer, they'd take long walks along the trails, often ending up at one of many secluded spots by the lake where they'd talk or sit in companionable silence.

She shook her head, trying to clear her mind. She

hadn't given much thought to Miles in years. Now that she was back in Aspen Creek, the memories of the times they'd shared had come flooding back. It didn't help that she'd seen him twice recently or that she could anticipate seeing him on a regular basis for the foreseeable future.

Despite trying to control her thoughts, she couldn't help thinking about the past.

It had been painful seeing him with a parade of women before. Knowing that he hadn't been in love with any of them had only been a slight comfort. Jillian had hoped that after dating all of those women, he'd realize that she was the one for him.

When he'd announced that he was getting married, that hope had died an agonizing death. Knowing that she'd never get over him in Aspen Creek, she'd moved to Kansas and become involved with Evan. She'd silenced the persistent voice that had nagged her, warning her that it was a mistake to marry him. Miles was moving on with his life and she needed to do the same thing. Her parents and brothers had tried to get her to slow things down, but to no avail. She'd been determined to marry if only to prove to herself that she was over Miles.

But she was back in Aspen Creek now. And there would be no avoiding him.

There was only one thing to do. She needed to keep herself so busy that she wouldn't have time to think about him. Though she hated to admit it, she knew it would be so easy to fall back into old habits and start hanging out with him. Oh, she wasn't still in love with him. He'd killed that feeling. Sure, she found him attractive—he was even better looking now than he'd been before—but love was more than liking the way a person looked. Or smelled. It was a commitment to each other—something he hadn't been willing to make then and that she wasn't going to make now. But she also knew that, despite her best intentions, she could easily fall in love with him, which would be a big mistake. They had walked that path before, and it had led to heartache for her and confusion for him.

The next day Jillian visited the resort. It had been a while since she'd worked there, and she wanted to familiarize herself with everything before her first day. More than that, she wanted to catch up with her former coworkers and friends and introduce herself to the employees she didn't know.

"Welcome back," the front desk manager said when Jillian stepped inside. Marion rounded the desk and gave Jillian a warm hug. She had been with the resort for as long as Jillian could remember. She was friendly and efficient, keeping the front desk running smoothly.

"It's good to be back," Jillian said, realizing that she meant it, despite her difficult feelings around Miles. "How's Trevor?"

Jillian had babysat Marion's son from time to time when he was younger. "Fine. He's in his senior year of high school and excited to start college in the fall."

"Wow. Already? How did he get so old so fast?"

"I ask myself that every day. You'll see, before you know it, your little girl will be starting school."

Jillian laughed. "Lilliana's still in diapers, so I have some time left. Where's Trevor going to school?"

"He has his heart set on Northwestern. I'm trying to get used to the idea of him being so far away."

"Oh. I foresee a lot of road trips in your future."

"You already know."

The phone rang and Marion hustled back behind the desk and picked up the phone.

Jillian waved goodbye and headed for the special events office, stopping to speak to the other employees she passed. When she reached the office, she stepped inside and looked around. She'd been a little bit nervous about returning to her old department, but everything looked the same and the feeling of familiarity surrounded her. There were a few new faces, but everyone seemed friendly. She'd always gotten along with her coworkers, who'd treated her like one of their crowd and not like the daughter of the owners.

"Jillian. I heard you were back. Sorry I missed your party. I took a nap after work and when I woke up it was morning."

Jillian smiled at Evie, one of her favorite co-workers. Evie and her husband, Brian, had been trying to have a baby for years. Jillian was glad to see that they had finally succeeded. "Being pregnant will do that. When are you due?"

"Not for three more months?"

"Really?"

Evie laughed. "Go ahead and say it. I'm huge."

Jillian shook her head. You couldn't pry those words past her lips with the jaws of life.

"I'm having twins if you can believe it."

Jillian hugged the other woman. "Congratulations."

"Two for the price of one."

Jillian chuckled. "You always did like a sale."

"Yep. I would love to chat more, but one of these babies is on my bladder, so…"

"No need to explain. We'll have to catch up later."

Jillian watched her friend waddle off to the ladies' room. She chatted with a few more friends and made plans to meet up soon. She was smiling with contentment as she left the resort and drove the short distance to the house. The sound of Lilliana's laughter greeted her as she stepped inside and took off her coat and boots.

"Guess who's home?" she called, following her daughter's voice to the kitchen.

"Mama. Hi Mama," Lilliana squealed and then

began squirming in her highchair, trying to get down.

"One second please," Valerie said, wiping her hands on her apron.

"I got her," Jillian said. In an instant she'd freed Lilliana from her chair and wrapped her in a tight hug. Lilliana giggled and then placed a sloppy kiss on Jillian's cheek. Laughing, Jillian tossed her daughter into the air, catching and kissing her again. Lilliana's joyous giggles made Jillian's heart soar. Although she'd enjoyed her afternoon at the resort, she'd missed Lilliana.

Jillian listened attentively as Lilliana "told" her of the fun she'd had with Grandma, picking out a few words like *toy* and *doll*. Lilliana pointed out the French doors to the patio and babbled some more.

"Is that right?" Jillian said although she only had a vague idea what Lilliana had said. Not that it mattered. The important thing was the joy that her daughter was showing as she talked about her day.

"That's right," Valerie added. "We went outside and built a snowman."

"Ball," Lilliana said, pushing against Jillian's chest in an attempt to get down. Jillian set her daughter on the floor and watched as she ran across the room as quickly as she could on her chubby little legs.

"I take it you played with the ball."

Valerie shook her head. "Not me. Your father."

"Dad?" Jillian asked in surprise. Her father was a serious businessman who rarely took time away from his office in the middle of the day. He'd been a good father, but he'd been determined to make the resort the best in the state so he could provide a good life for his family. As a result, he'd missed meals and several school functions. Valerie had insisted that he be there for Sunday dinner with the family no matter the season or how busy it was at the resort. And when they'd begun to host weddings, bridal receptions and other big events on the property, Wednesday had always been excluded. Those evenings had been reserved exclusively for family.

Henry might have missed a few events, but when he'd been present, he'd been *present*. As a result, he had a strong relationship with all of his children. Even so, Jillian was surprised that he'd left work in the middle of the day today.

"I know what you're thinking. Your father is just as committed to the resort as ever, but Grant has been taking on more responsibility, freeing up your father. And there's something special about having a grandchild in the house. They change your priorities."

"And rules," Jillian added.

"You know it." Valerie showed no shame at how relaxed she was with Lilliana. The rules that she'd made her kids live by didn't apply to Lilliana. As busy owners of a thriving resort, they hadn't had a lot of free time to spare and had needed to know where their children were and what they were doing. Jillian, Marty, Victor and Grant had designated chores at home that they had been expected to perform. When they'd been old enough, they'd taken jobs at the resort. Grant had loved it and had always planned to take over the business when their father retired. Now it looked like that time was coming sooner than Jillian expected.

Henry had insisted that, to run the company, Grant needed to know what each person did and why. He'd worked in every position over the years, and, after receiving a business degree from Harvard, he had become vice president. Marty, Victor and Jillian had taken their jobs seriously, but they hadn't wanted to make a career out of it. Marty had enjoyed cooking and had created a line of barbecue sauce that was sold in stores across the country. He had a popular restaurant on the premises of the resort and was opening a second in town. He also catered special events on occasion.

Victor had stepped away from the hospitality field altogether and was a firefighter in Denver.

Jillian was proud of her brothers, but unlike them, she hadn't found her niche before getting married and having a child. While her brothers had been busy building their careers, she'd been focused on her relationship with Miles. Her parents had insisted that she go to college, something for which she was eternally grateful. She'd gotten a degree in hotel management with a minor in accounting. When Lilliana was older, Jillian would put that degree to use, but right now she was happy with a less demanding position.

Sometimes late at night, she wondered what her life would have turned out like if she hadn't been so wrapped up in Miles. What if she would have been as business oriented as her brothers? Would she have been as devastated when Miles told her that he didn't want to get married? Would she have gotten involved with Evan on the rebound and then ignored all of her parents' warnings about making a decision without giving it proper thought? She truthfully didn't know. The only thing that kept her from wanting to go back and change things was the love she had for her daughter. And given the bitterness she harbored in her heart, her reluctance to become involved with another man and the resistance she felt to a romantic relationship at any time in the future, that love would have to be enough to sustain her.

"Speaking of rules," Jillian said, deciding that she'd had more than enough introspection for the day, "I guess I should help with dinner."

"That would be nice. I miss having help with meals."

"I'm no Marty," Jillian reminded herself.

"Who is?"

Jillian and her mother laughed as they got down to work. Jillian hadn't been interested in cooking as a girl, but over time she'd learned. When they set dinner on the table that evening, she held her breath as her father tasted her pot roast.

"Five stars," he said. "Just as good as Marty's."

"You're lying, which makes me know I'm your favorite child."

"Definitely my favorite daughter."

She picked up the spoon and held it up to Lilliana's mouth. "Come on. How about you eat some?"

Lilliana shook her head and pressed her lips together. Clearly she wasn't in the mood for peas and carrots.

"Why don't you let me take over and you eat your own food," her father said. "Then you go and relax while I have some time with my special girl."

"That sounds nice. If you don't mind."

"Mind? Why would I mind?" Her father picked Lilliana out of her highchair and set her onto his lap. She lay her head on his shoulder and gave him a big grin. "Who's hungry?"

"Me." Lilliana pointed to her chest. When Henry brought the spoon closer to her lips, she grabbed it and shoved it into her mouth. Then she took the spoon and began to feed herself.

"Little stinker," Jillian muttered.

"You were the same way," her mother said. "I

would just about pull out my hair trying to get you to eat. Nothing worked. Then your dad would hold you and you'd become an eating machine."

"I've got the magic touch," he bragged.

"And the c-o-o-k-i-e-s," Valerie retorted.

"Whatever works," he said.

No wonder Lilliana wouldn't eat for Jillian. She was holding out for treats. Jillian supposed an oatmeal raisin cookie after dinner wouldn't hurt.

They laughed as they ate. By the time they had finished dinner, Jillian's soul was as full as her stomach.

"You look nice," Valerie said when Jillian stepped downstairs holding Lilliana by the hand two days later. They were dressed and ready to go to playgroup.

"Thanks." Jillian didn't bother pretending that she hadn't taken extra time with her appearance today. The previous two times she'd seen Miles, she'd been caught off guard and as a result she hadn't looked her best. When he'd popped up unannounced and uninvited at her house, she'd been wearing her most comfortable jeans and a heavy sweater designed more for warmth than fashion. Her hair had been pulled into a messy ponytail and she hadn't been wearing any makeup. Her appearance had been slightly better when she'd gone to playgroup. She'd been presentable but Miles had easily outshined her.

He'd been dressed in jeans and a flannel shirt that had emphasized his broad shoulders and muscular chest. She'd had a hard time not staring at him, but she'd managed. The last thing she wanted was for him to think that she was still attracted to him.

Today she was wearing dark jeans and a waist-length red sweater. She'd left her hair loose, and the curls bounced around her shoulders. She'd brushed on a bit of mascara and dabbed on lipstick. She'd added hoop earrings and several bangles on each wrist. She wasn't trying to look like a fashion model, but she did want to look nice.

"Does your appearance have anything to do with Miles?" Valerie asked perceptively.

"Maybe a little bit. I know it's petty, but I want him to get a good look at what he walked away from. I want him to see what he's missing."

Valerie laughed. "I think he already knows that. I'm not saying that he regretted his marriage, but I know you meant a lot to him. And that he missed you and your friendship. And it has nothing to do with how beautiful you are. It's because of the person you are on the inside. The connection that the two of you shared."

Jillian looked down at herself. "You think I'm overdoing it?"

Valerie shrugged. "I've always felt that when I

look my best, I'm more confident. And it's not as if you're wearing a strand of pearls."

Jillian smiled. She could always count on her mother to wipe away any insecurities she had. She helped Lilliana into her coat and then put on her own jacket. "See you later, Mom."

"Have fun," Valerie replied as Jillian and Lilliana left.

Jillian turned on a children's CD as they drove to the library. Lilliana began singing and clapping along to the music. Jillian pointed out landmarks occasionally, and Lilliana bobbed her head. Jillian wasn't sure whether she was nodding to her or keeping time to the music. Either way, it made the drive fun. Jillian was getting Lilliana out of her car seat when Miles parked next to her. By the time she had Lilliana situated, Benji and Miles were standing beside them.

"Hi," Miles said, smiling. It was as if he had forgotten her coolness the other day and they were once more the best of friends. Jillian couldn't decide whether she should be annoyed or admire his ability to act as if everything was normal.

"Hi," Lilliana replied. As friendly as ever, she took two small steps and reached out to grab Benji's hand. "Hi, Enji."

"Hi, Lily."

Lilliana giggled, clearly pleased to be interacting with her new best friend.

Miles looked from the children to Jillian. "Shall we go inside?"

She hadn't intended to spend time with him today, but from the way their children had glued themselves to each other she knew she didn't have a choice. Even so, she was going to jump at the first chance she had to ditch him.

"Sure." She took Lilliana's free hand while Miles took Benji's. The four of them must have looked like a family as they walked together across the snowy lot. Jillian forced that thought from her mind before it could settle in and get comfortable. She'd fantasized herself into a broken heart years ago. She could blame that mistake on youth, but she was older and wiser now. She wouldn't engage in that same foolishness anymore.

"You look nice, by the way," Miles said after they'd stepped inside and removed their coats. His eyes traveled over her from head to toes.

"This old thing?" she said with a grin. When she realized her comment could have been taken as flirting, she frowned and turned away.

"Uh-oh. Can't have that," Miles said, deadpan.

"Can't have what?"

"You being nice to me. Treating me like a human being. It completely ruins this whole you-and-me-being-enemies thing you have going."

"I don't have any sort of thing going on."

"Really?" He raised his eyebrows, letting that one word hang between them. She'd forgotten how good he was at communicating an entire paragraph with one word and a bit of body language.

"Go play?" Lilliana asked. Jillian nodded.

The kids made a beeline for the pile of blocks in the middle of the room. Jillian was tempted to follow them, leaving Miles in her dust. But she couldn't. Not with his accusation hanging in the air. No way was she letting him have the last word.

"I don't think we're enemies," she said.

He scoffed. "Come on. You're treating me like the villain and you know it."

"You're certainly not the hero you pretend to be."

"I'm not pretending to be anything." His usually calm voice was slightly raised and filled with emotion. "I'm just a regular guy trying to make it through the day. I get up early, go to work and take care of my son. When I go to bed at night, I hope that I've done everything to the best of my ability but somehow feel that I haven't. That I've somehow failed my son even if I can't put my finger on how."

She hadn't expected him to be so open. So transparent about his insecurities. She nodded reluctantly. She understood the doubt that he was describing. The uncertainty that being a single parent brought even though she hadn't been the one to end the marriage. Evan had. Not that he'd been much of a partner.

But it wasn't only the doubt about raising Lilliana that troubled Jillian. It was the fear of repeating past mistakes that kept her tossing and turning in her bed at night.

"And I know that I hurt you," Miles was saying, pulling Jillian's attention back to the conversation. "You wouldn't accept my apology back then, but years have passed and hopefully emotions have cooled. So I'll ask again. Will you please forgive me for hurting you? That was never my intention."

She knew he was sincere and that the mature thing to do was accept his apology. But she couldn't. Clearly he didn't understand how badly he'd hurt her, as evidenced by this bland speech. "I don't know why you need me to accept your apology. After all, you don't think you did anything wrong."

"I never lied to you. I didn't sneak around behind your back."

"That's a pretty low bar."

"That being said, I should have been up front about my doubts when I started having them instead of blindsiding you. We'd been together forever. I wasn't sure it had been for the right reasons. I wanted to be sure it was out of love and not out of habit. You deserved a man who was sure."

"And then while you were exploring your options, Rachel got pregnant."

"One night of stupidity on my part changed all of our lives."

"One night?" That was a surprise. She shouldn't have felt comforted hearing that, but somehow she was.

"Yes. She was here on vacation. You know, what happens on vacation stays on vacation. Except it didn't. When she told me she was pregnant, I knew I had to do the right thing. No matter who it hurt."

"Thanks for confirming what I already knew. My feelings meant very little to you." Jillian couldn't keep the bitterness from her voice.

Miles shoved his hands into his jeans pockets. "I give up. I was trying to explain what happened and how I ended up married to Rachel. I'm sorry that we can't put it behind us and start over now. You were the best friend I ever had and I've missed having you in my life. I thought of you over the years and hoped that you were happy. Don't worry. I get the message and I won't bother you again."

"That would be for the best," she said, hoping that they had finally put the subject and their relationship to bed at last.

Benji and Lilliana laughed and Jillian and Miles turned and looked in their direction. She and Miles might not be friends any longer, but Benji and Lilliana were getting along like old pals. Lilliana was a friendly little girl but she hadn't gotten attached to any one child in the past. Generally she'd played with whomever happened to be in her vicinity. Jillian had hoped that would be the case with Benji and that Lilliana would choose another kid to play with today. But Lilliana and Benji appeared glued to each other's sides.

"Come on, Daddy," Benji called to Miles.

Lilliana grinned and gave a backward wave to Jillian. Miles glanced at Jillian and she gave him a rueful smile. Clearly they were going to be stuck with each other for the time being. They joined the children as they played, keeping as much distance between them as possible, which wasn't much. Benji had taken a while to warm up to Jillian last time, preferring to play with Lilliana. Today he was much friendlier, handing Jillian a colorful block to add to the tower he and Lilliana were building.

"Thank you," Jillian said, placing the blue block on the top of the teetering tower, taking the moment to straighten some of the wobbling plastic.

Benji smiled and then handed her another block. "Give it to Daddy."

Jillian bit back a sigh and then turned to Miles, who'd watched the entire interaction without saying a word. His face was unreadable, and she mourned the lost days when she knew what he was feeling just from the expression on his face. Or by the way he tapped his foot or drummed his fingers against his thigh. But that would require her to let down

her guard and let him in, something she was unwilling to do.

"Give it to Daddy so he can play, too," Benji com-
manded a little more urgently when Jillian didn't
move as quickly as he liked.

"Sure." She forced a smile and gave the piece to
Miles, being careful not to brush his hand. When
Miles shook his head, a crooked grin on his face,
she knew she hadn't been as subtle as she'd hoped.
But then subtlety had never been her strong suit.
She'd always been bold and daring, outgoing with
her opinions and clear about her expectations.

But, exasperated about being caught avoiding
contact, she grabbed his hand and placed the block
into it. As expected, there was a zing of electricity when they touched. Even now, after all that had
passed between them, her body still reacted to his.
Oh, it wasn't as strong as it had been years ago, but
it was still noticeable enough to be worrying.

"Thank you." His voice was slightly hoarse, and
she wondered if it was because he'd felt the same
tingle she had. She forced that thought away. How
many times did she have to warn herself of the dan-
gers he presented before she remembered to keep
her heart protected from him? Because even if he
was still attracted to her—something she doubted—
she knew it didn't go any further than that. He'd
been wild for her when they were younger, but he
hadn't wanted to make a lifetime commitment.

She'd be a fool to think that anything had changed since then.

It shouldn't be this hard to keep her feelings for Miles in the past. She hadn't thought about Evan since he'd announced that marriage wasn't as much fun as he'd thought it would be and then walked out on her and Lilliana. If she ran into him in the future, she doubted she'd be close to swooning like she was right this moment. So why was she still vulnerable to Miles?

Okay, so he was good-looking in a rugged kind of way. He'd never been traditionally handsome, but there was something about the shape of his nose, the deep brown of his eyes and his full lips that had always appealed to her. And it probably always would. But she knew better than to let attraction get the better of her.

"Play with us," Benji demanded, and Lilliana echoed that sentiment with a charming smile that could melt the coldest heart.

"Sure," Miles said, getting more comfortable on the floor. Doing so brought him even closer to Jillian, and his clean, masculine scent surrounded her. It would be foolish to try to hold her breath for twenty minutes, so she continued to breathe naturally, getting a whiff of him every time she inhaled.

They all played together until it was story time for the kids. Miles and Jillian joined the other parents in the adjoining room. When Jillian spotted

Lauren, she immediately excused herself and joined her friend.

"So, you and Miles again?" Lauren asked, her eyes gleaming with mischief.

"Not in this lifetime."

"Really? The four of you looked so cute together. Like a little family."

Jillian's heart lurched at her friend's words, which echoed her own earlier thoughts. "Don't even start. And why didn't you tell me that he and his son were a part of this playgroup?"

"Did you forget rule number one? Under no circumstances am I ever to mention his name to you for fear of losing our friendship."

"Still. I would think you'd make an exception using the things-I-need-to-know clause."

"I didn't know such a clause existed. Besides, what difference does it make now? Or are you still in love with the man?"

"That's a definite no. And forewarned is forearmed."

"Were you planning on going to war with him? It certainly didn't look like that way from where I sat, watching like a hawk and taking notes to share with our friends."

"No. And that's not what I meant."

"Besides, he didn't know you would be here, either."

Jillian nodded. "Wait a minute. What do you mean you plan to talk about me to our friends?"

Lauren laughed. "Surely you don't expect me to keep all of this juicy gossip to myself. I expect my phone to be buzzing by the time I get home."

"Nosy friends are the worst."

"Speaking of nosy friends, we're having a girls' night out this Saturday. We try to get together at least once a month. This time we're meeting at Grady's for drinks and dancing. Will you be able to come?"

"Let me check with my mother and see if she'll be able to babysit. I'm living with my parents now and I don't want to take advantage."

"I completely understand that. But if your mother is anything like mine, she'll love having Lilliana to herself to spoil."

"I don't doubt it. She's already erased so many rules that my brothers and I had to live with that I just shake my head. And my father is only slightly better."

They laughed together and Jillian once more was glad that she'd decided to return home. Although she'd made friends in Kansas, none of them could replace the lifetime relationships she had here in Aspen Creek. You couldn't make old friends. When she and Lilliana left playgroup that day with Miles and Benji, Jillian was in a better mood. She even managed to smile at Miles.

When he returned her smile, butterflies danced in her stomach. No. She wasn't going there. Once more she reminded herself that what she and Miles had once shared was over and done with. There was no going back.

So why did his smile make her feel warm all over?

Chapter Five

Miles heard his doorbell ring a moment before the front door opened.

"Anybody here?" Isaac called.

"You are so not funny," Nathan's voice was humorless and slightly annoyed.

"I'm in the kitchen," Miles called back moments before his brothers stepped inside. "What are you doing here?"

"We've come to rescue you from yet another weekend of boredom," Isaac said. "Grab your coat. We're going to Grady's."

"You don't say?" Miles folded his arms over his chest. He'd expect something like this from Isaac who spent every free moment at the club or with one woman or another. But Nathan? This was completely out of character for him. Nathan would rather work than do just about anything.

Miles glanced at his older brother who only shrugged. "This wasn't my idea."

"And yet you're here."

"A meeting was canceled. And what can I say, Isaac caught me at a weak moment. I was going to turn him down, but he made a good point."

"Which is?"

"You spend every free moment with Benji. You need to get out and have some fun."

"Spoken by the man dressed in a suit who is only going out because a meeting was canceled."

"Thanks for the summary," Isaac said. "Now grab your coat and let's go."

"Benji –"

" – is spending the night with Mom baking cookies." Isaac smirked.

"You set that up." Michelle had called a few minutes ago to let Miles know that she wanted Benji to sleep over. He'd planned to use the time to get caught up on the endless loads of laundry and maybe watch some TV.

"Thank me later."

"I haven't said I was coming,"

"Come on man, you have a free night. You can polish the silver or whatever the hell boring thing you were going to do at some other time."

Nathan shook his head. "I hate to say this twice in the same night, but he's right."

"Yay me," Isaac said. He crossed the floor and grabbed Miles's hat and jacket from the hook. "Let's go. There are women to meet. If you play your cards right, you guys might end up with one who prefers you to me."

Miles looked at the jacket and cowboy hat in his brother's hand. Isaac's eyes held challenge. It *had* been a while since he'd gone out. And Benji was being cared for. He supposed it wouldn't hurt to go out tonight.

"Fine," he said, taking the hat from his brother and then setting it on his head. "But don't do anything to make me regret it."

Isaac laughed. "Only the two of you could regret having a good time."

Jillian inhaled deeply before stepping out of her car. It had been ages since she'd had a night to herself. When she and Evan had first been married, it had been all about them as a couple. And truth be told, they generally did things that Evan wanted to do. Once Lilliana had come along, Jillian had been in mom mode. Although Evan had still spent time with his friends, he hadn't been interested in watching Lilliana so Jillian could spend time with hers.

Now she stood outside Grady's, taking in Aspen Creek after dark. The town was quieter than it was during the day when vacationers bustled about, going from boutique to boutique. The shops had closed a couple of hours ago, not that there were any fancy stores on this block. This side of town was where the locals shopped and partied. The buildings were just as well-kept and the streets just as clean as Main Street. But if you didn't know about this club, you wouldn't find it.

"Hey, Jillian."

Jillian turned and saw Lauren hurrying in her direction. "You look so great."

"So do you."

They were both wearing big coats open to reveal short skirts and cute tops.

They stepped into the club and looked around. Erica stood up from a table where she and Courtney were sitting and then waved at them. Jillian and Lauren crossed the room and joined them. A waitress came over and immediately took their drink orders.

Jillian looked around the club. It wasn't so much a pickup place as a gathering spot for locals, which suited Jillian and her friends just fine. They weren't interested in meeting men tonight. They just wanted to have fun.

Although Jillian was divorced with a child, her friends were single with no children. The last time Jillian had been around, Courtney had been engaged, but other than saying things hadn't worked out, she hadn't brought up her ex again. Having two failed relationships that Jillian would prefer not to discuss, she understood completely.

They were still laughing and talking twenty minutes later when the door opened and a group of people walked in. Jillian's back was to the door, but when her friends stopped talking and stared at the entrance, she turned around to see who had attracted their attention.

Miles.

What was he doing here? He was standing between his brothers and hadn't spotted her yet. She took a moment to look at him. Dressed in dark jeans, a leather jacket and a white pullover that contrasted nicely with his rich brown skin and fit his muscular body perfectly, he looked absolutely gorgeous. Despite the fact that she was working hard to remain immune to him, her heart skipped a beat. She wanted to look away, but her eyes were glued to him. It was as if she were caught under his spell that she was powerless to break.

Miles looked in her direction, catching her staring at him. For a moment their eyes held and time stopped. Erica kicked Jillian's foot, knocking her out of her stupor.

"Why did you kick me?"

"You were staring so hard, I thought you might bore a hole into his chest. The last thing I want to do on my first night off in a while is perform surgery."

"First, you're an ER doctor, not a surgeon, and second, I wasn't looking that hard."

"Yes, you were," Lauren chimed in and Courtney nodded in agreement.

"Well, I'm just surprised to see him. Please tell me you didn't know he'd be here."

"No," Lauren quickly assured her. "We've come here a few times and have never seen him once."

"In fact, it's very rare to see him in town at all," Courtney added. "At least not socializing. He's a very devoted father and the only time I see him is with his son."

"So he's not dating?" Jillian asked then immediately wanted to bite her tongue. She didn't care if he was seeing every woman in Aspen Creek and their out-of-town cousins.

Her friends glanced at each other, smiles on their faces. The wheels were turning in their heads; they were plotting something. She was going to have to nip any sort of plan in the bud. The cockamamie schemes they'd come up with as teenagers had been fun and harmless, but they were all adults now. Their actions had major consequences.

"I don't think so, but we can call him over and ask," Courtney said, a mischievous grin on her face.

"Don't even think about it," Jillian warned. "I don't really care."

"No?" Lauren asked dubiously.

"No," Jillian said firmly. "It's just that his son and my daughter have become fast friends at playgroup, so we end up thrown together. I don't want anyone thinking I'm trying to move in on their man. I don't need that kind of drama in my life."

"No, I imagine you wouldn't. But you don't have to worry about a crazed girlfriend coming after you. That is, if that is your sincere concern." Erica winked, letting Jillian know she hadn't fooled anyone. Old friends were great, and she was grateful for hers, but sometimes they were too perceptive.

"He looks good, but his brother Isaac looks much better in my opinion," Courtney said. "There's something about a man with a beard and locs that does it for me."

"Really? You like Isaac love-'em-and-leave-'em Montgomery?" Erica said, wrinkling her nose.

"I believe he's called Isaac love-'em-and-leave-'em-*happy* Montgomery," Courtney corrected with a laugh. "I think commitment is overrated, but I'm up for a night of fun."

"Don't look now, but they're on their way over here," Lauren said, jostling Jillian's shoulder.

Please, no, Jillian thought to herself. This was supposed to be a fun night out with her friends where she could relax and let down her hair. A time when they could laugh and tease each other. Having Miles around would totally ruin that.

"Hi," Isaac said, flashing a thousand-watt smile as the three brothers stepped up to the table.

Jillian and her friends echoed the greeting. Miles looked slightly uncomfortable, as if coming over to the table hadn't been his idea but he'd been out-voted. Seeing his discomfort made hers more bear-able. It was good to know that she wasn't alone in wanting to have time to enjoy herself.

"Jillian, it's good to see you," Nathan said, lean-ing over to kiss her cheek.

"You, too," Jillian said sincerely. Nathan had al-ways been friendly to her when she and Miles had dated. She'd never forget how kind he'd been to her after the breakup. He'd bluntly told her that Miles was an idiot and that he was still her friend. She could feel free to call him whenever she wanted.

"We'd better grab a table," Miles said abruptly.

Nathan gave Miles a long look and then smiled to himself as if suddenly amused.

"We'll see you ladies later," Isaac said, his smile pure charm.

Jillian watched them walk away, not breathing easily until Miles had sat down at a table across the room.

"You can relax," Lauren said. "He's not coming back over here."

"Although his brother sure could," Courtney said.

"Girls' night out. Remember?" Jillian said.

"Yes. But if he asks me to dance later, I'm going to."

"That's acceptable," Erica said. "But until then, it's just us."

* * *

"Did you know Jillian was going to be here?" Miles asked, the moment they were sitting at their table. He looked from one brother to the other. He didn't think they'd set him up like this, but you could never know for sure.

"Of course," Isaac said. "She always clears her schedule with me."

Miles glared at him.

"You're serious?" Isaac said. When Miles didn't laugh, he sobered. "No, I didn't know she would be here. How would I? I haven't seen her since she's been back in town."

"Neither have I," Nathan added. "I was out of town and missed her party."

Miles swallowed his unexpected jealousy that Nathan had been invited to Jillian's party and he hadn't been.

"You're just paranoid because she's been on your mind," Isaac said.

"No, I'm not and no, she hasn't been."

"Then what's the problem? Who cares if she's here or not? It's Saturday night and the place is filled with beautiful women. Women who are looking for fun. Fun I am more than willing to provide," Isaac said.

"There's no problem," Miles clarified. At least there shouldn't be. He was here to have fun.

Miles was the first to admit that he'd become a

bit of a hermit these past couple of years. It hadn't been deliberate, but it had happened nonetheless. After the way his marriage had ended, he wasn't eager to jump into the dating pool again. But even he knew there was a big difference between looking for love and having a fun night out with his brothers. And he had been enjoying himself until he'd crashed headlong into his past. Again.

Jillian was back in town and she was becoming part of his present whether or not either of them liked it. A part of him wondered what could have been. What would their lives look like if they had stayed together? Would they be happy together or would they regret never having dated other people? He would never know so there was no sense in torturing himself.

Once he and his brothers had decided on their drinks, Miles went up to the bar to put in the order. While he was waiting for the bartender to fill it, his eyes were drawn to the table where Jillian sat with her friends. She was in profile, and he took the time to look at her. As usual, her gorgeous hair was flowing down her back, and it bounced when she moved her head. One of her friends said something that made the rest of them burst into laughter. Jillian tossed her head and then brushed her hair behind her ear with a slender hand. She wasn't wearing a ring, but she had on a few bangles that moved and he could imagine the sound they'd make as they knocked against each other.

She was wearing a gold top that looked like heaven against her brown skin. Her legs were hidden beneath the table, and he longed for the chance to see them up close.

"Here you are," the bartender said, setting three bottles of beer on the oak bar.

"Thanks." He handed over some cash and then walked back to the table. The place was loud, but in a few minutes the house band would begin to play their set and conversation would fade as people watched the show. After that, the DJ would take over and the dance floor would be packed.

"I was beginning to think we were going to have to send a search party to find you," Isaac said, taking a beer from Miles.

"The line was long," Miles said.

"And you were too busy staring at Jillian to notice when the bartender put the beers down the first time," Nathan said.

"You know, you could have gotten your own drinks," Miles said.

"Or you could have let that cute waitress take our order," Isaac said. "But then you wouldn't have been able to stare at Jillian."

"You guys are making me regret not sitting on the couch at home alone tonight. It's beginning to sound a lot more appealing."

"Don't let them get to you. It's hard stepping back into the dating pool after being gone for so long," came a voice from behind him.

Miles turned around and looked into the face of his friend Josh Wilson. "Hey."

"Mind if I join you?"

"Please do," Miles said, pushing out a chair. "I'm feeling outnumbered here."

Josh laughed as he sat down. Josh had been separated from his wife for two years. Oddly enough, neither he nor his wife seemed interested in taking the steps necessary to dissolve the marriage. Miles wasn't sure if Josh and Krissy would ever get divorced or if they even wanted to. But since they seemed happy living their lives in limbo, who was he to judge? Miles certainly was no expert on marriage.

They kidded around for a while and Miles began to relax. He'd missed hanging out. He'd felt so guilty about the divorce and raising Benji without a mother. As a result, he'd devoted every spare minute to his son. He'd always known that he needed time to unwind, but it seemed unfair to expect his mother to watch Benji while he was out enjoying himself.

"She's still there," Nathan said, bumping Miles with his elbow. Isaac and Josh had gotten up and were talking with a couple of women, so he and Miles were alone.

Miles realized he hadn't been as subtle as he'd thought. Breathing out a long breath, he took one last look at Jillian before returning his attention to his brother. "I don't know what's wrong with me. Jillian and I were over a long time ago. And to be honest, she's been pretty cold to me. She's made it clear that she doesn't want to be friends again."

"What do you want?"

"I have no idea." Miles took a pull of his beer and then set the bottle back on the table. "I mean, I wasn't hoping that we could pick up where we left off. We haven't seen each other in years and our lives are so different than they were years ago. We've each been married and divorced. We're single parents. To be honest, we don't even know each other now. There are so many reasons a relationship wouldn't work."

"Are you trying to convince me or yourself?"

He huffed out a wry laugh. "I don't know. Just between the two of us, I was glad when I heard that Jillian was moving back to town. I missed her and I wanted to find a way to be friends. But I wasn't hoping the two of us would get back together again."

"But?"

"No buts."

"She's certainly beautiful."

Miles heard the appreciation in Nathan's voice and an unexpected wave of jealousy swept over him. Nathan had always told Miles that he was making a mistake by letting Jillian go. Was Nathan suddenly interested in Jillian? Reminding himself that Jillian didn't belong to him—heck, she didn't even like him—he shoved the jealousy away. The last thing he wanted was to hassle with his brother over a woman who wasn't his and hadn't been for years. He grunted a response.

"Don't worry, Miles, I'm not interested in her. Never was. Besides, I saw the way the two of you ignored each other."

"What does that even mean?"

"It means that there might still be something between the two of you."

"Trust me. There isn't."

"So you won't be upset if I ask her out."

Miles's eyes narrowed. "No. She's free to date whoever she wants to date."

Nathan nodded. After a moment, he smiled. "Just kidding. She's gorgeous and all, but like I said, I'm not interested. We're brothers, Miles. Brothers don't date each other's exes."

Miles smiled, trying to understand the relief that surged through him.

Josh and Isaac returned to the table and the conversation switched to sports and Isaac's favorite topic: women.

"There are some great looking women here tonight," Isaac said.

"I take it you found your date for the rest of the night?" Miles asked.

"I've narrowed it down to two. I'll dance with each of them and then decide. I need to make sure she has rhythm."

"You are so shallow," Nathan said.

"And you're too serious," Isaac replied. "Not to mention judgmental." Isaac smirked. "I guess I did mention it."

Nathan frowned and looked like he was about to retort when the band took the stage. Thank goodness. Miles didn't feel like refereeing at the moment. He stood and joined the others as they gathered around the stage to watch the show.

Miles wasn't sure how it happened, but he and his friends ended up standing next to Jillian and her friends. And he and Jillian were side by side, their shoulders brushing. If he didn't know better, he'd think his brothers and her friends were in cahoots, determined to get the former lovers back together.

He and Jillian's friends had gone to school together. If he recalled correctly, they'd always had an extra dose of romance in their hearts, so their behavior was understandable. But his brothers and Josh? There was absolutely no excuse for their behavior. They were pushing him and Jillian together in an attempt to get under his skin. He would have to prove to them that their mind games weren't going to work.

He turned and smiled at Jillian. It wasn't planned and didn't take much effort. Smiling at Jillian was as natural as breathing. "This band is really good."

She smiled in return. Despite the fact that he was only engaging in conversation to show how unbothered he was by her, his heart skipped a beat.

"Yes. It's nice to see that Grady's still has good bands."

"Still? Don't tell me you forgot the band that one summer?"

Her eyes filled with mirth a few seconds before she burst into laughter. "Oh, my goodness. I don't think I could forget them if I live to be a hundred. They were horrible. The lead singer had to be the worst singer I've ever heard. And given that I can't carry a tune with a handle on it, that's saying something."

Miles and Jillian had just turned twenty-one that summer and had become regulars at the club. The owners had been hyping a band from Georgia, so Miles and Jillian had come to see them. By the time the band started their second song, it had become clear that the music was going to be terrible.

Miles laughed. "I still think someone in the band had to be related to one of the owners because there is no way they heard them audition and thought, *yeah, these guys are headliners*."

Jillian shook her head. "When did you become a conspiracy theorist?"

"Like you didn't think the same thing."

"Think? After the second song, I lost the ability to perform higher functions like thinking. I was only trying to survive."

"I remember. Luckily we won't have to go screaming into the night this time."

She held up a foot. She was wearing ankle-high boots with four-inch heels that showcased her sexy calves. "Good thing. I don't think I can run in these."

"But are you able to dance in them?"

"I should be. Why?"

He held out a hand. The band had finished their up-tempo song and had segued into a ballad. Several couples were on the dance floor swaying to the music and Miles hoped that he and Jillian could join them. "Why waste this good music?"

She hesitated, and while she deliberated, he realized just how badly he wanted her to say yes. Not because he wanted to prove to himself that he was over Jillian. Rather because he wanted to hold her in his arms and feel her body pressed against him. To inhale her sweet scent again.

She placed her hand in his and he blew out a relieved breath.

He pulled her into his arms as he'd done so many times in this very club. She leaned against him and it felt so familiar—so right—that the past few years might have been mere minutes. Jillian was a graceful dancer, and as they swayed together to the saxophone, he closed his eyes and let the music carry him away to a place where all was right in the world. A place where he and Jillian were no longer at odds.

He had begun to worry that he'd burned the bridge between them, leaving them no way to get back to a good place. Now he wasn't as pessimistic. He knew it wouldn't be easy for them to become friends again. He would have to win back Jillian's trust, which would be no easy feat. But as the warmth from her body wrapped around him, there was nothing that he wanted more in the world.

That ballad melted into another and they continued to dance. With each step they took, Miles grew more certain that things would work out between them.

The lead singer sang the last note of the song before the drummer banged out a solo and the band launched into an up-tempo number that had the crowd roaring. Jillian backed away from Miles, creating a distance between them—and not just physically. He yearned to pull her into his arms again, but there was no way to reclaim the previous closeness. The magic between them had vanished, leaving only cold reality behind. Jillian started to turn, but he grabbed her hand, unwilling to pretend the moment hadn't happened. He refused to allow Jillian to act as if their relationship hadn't shifted. A few slow dances might not seem monumental in the great scheme of things, but they'd shared a pleasant moment. They could build on that. That was a big deal to him.

"Thanks for the dances," he said, when the silence between them grew.

"You're welcome." She twisted her fingers, a sign that she was uncomfortable. She was rarely uncomfortable—and never with him. His heart ached when he realized just how much their relationship had disintegrated.

She took a step away from the dance floor and he quickly fell in beside her. She glanced at him quizzically and he shrugged. "We're going in the same direction so we may as well walk together."

"If you say so."

He decided to go for broke. "It's good to see you, Jillian. Dancing with you felt just like old times."

She inhaled deeply and headed for a secluded corner, gesturing for him to follow her. When they were alone, she looked at him, her expression somber. "We can't go back to where we were before. Too much has happened between us. We're different people now."

"I know that. And to be honest, I wouldn't change the past few years if I could. That would mean erasing my son, which I could never do."

"I feel the same about my daughter."

"But there's nothing saying we can't be friends again, is there?"

"Miles," she said and then paused. His heart sank. Then she blew out a long breath. "I suppose we could be friends again. After all, our kids like each other."

"That's true. And Benji is a quiet kid who generally plays alone." Miles had been worried about his son's social skills. Michelle had claimed that Miles had been the same way as a kid and had eventually grown out of it. That hadn't been entirely true, and his mother's words hadn't been as comforting as she'd intended. It wasn't until Jillian had burst into his life and had dragged him into her circle that he'd begun to interact with others.

"Like father like son," she joked.

"There's no denying that." Truth be told, there were still times when he preferred his own company. But these days, he was beginning to look forward to spending more time with Jillian.

"Not only in personality. He looks exactly like you."

Miles nodded. His mother had shown him pictures of himself when he was Benji's age. The resemblance was uncanny, even for a father and son. Even so, Miles hoped that Benji grew up with more confidence than he'd had as a child and teenager. His life would be so much easier that way. As soon as Miles had the thought, he shoved it away. His parents had never attempted to change his personality. They'd let him be himself. He would be just as accepting with Benji.

"I know. And might I say the same thing about Lilliana? It's like going back in time and seeing a little Jillian."

"Believe me, I know. That girl is always on. I'm lucky if I get a moment of silence. Mom swears that she's the child I deserve."

"You were always thinking of things for us to do. I doubt that anyone else in town had the ability to find so many creative ways of getting into trouble."

"Now you're just being mean," she said and then poked his shoulder.

He laughed. "Maybe. But where's the lie?"

She shook her head. "I guess there isn't one."

Before they could continue their conversation, someone passed by, and Jillian leaned away from him. Once the person was gone, she kept her distance. It was a subtle thing, but Miles noticed. "I should get back to my friends. And you should get back with your brothers."

He wanted to keep talking, but he knew the moment between them was gone. He didn't let that fact dampen his mood. Jillian had agreed to be his friend. And that was progress.

Chapter Six

Jillian checked on Lilliana and then climbed into bed. Tonight had been more fun than she'd expected. She'd spent time with her friends at her homecoming party a couple of weeks ago, but she'd needed to circulate, so they hadn't had the chance to kick back and let their hair down.

Tonight they had. It had just been the four of them, like it had been in high school and the summers when they'd all been home from college. She and Miles might still be fumbling about, trying to pick up the pieces of their relationship, but that hadn't been a problem with her girlfriends. However, there wasn't any bad blood between them like there was with Miles.

Miles. As hard as she tried not to, she couldn't

stop thinking of how good it had felt to be in his arms while they'd danced. It had been heavenly. Almost like a dream. The years had been good to him. His chest was hard and well-developed. His arms were thick and powerful. Incredibly, he seemed more manly now than he'd been years ago.

"You are ridiculous," she muttered to herself. If he seemed different tonight, it was because she wasn't looking at him through a haze of anger and disappointment. She was simply seeing him as he was.

She was glad they'd buried the proverbial hatchet. Being angry with him was exhausting. It took a lot of effort to resist him and remember that they weren't friends. And keeping her distance from him was impossible, given that their children were in the same playgroup and liked each other so much. Of course, Lilliana liked everyone, and everyone adored her, so her friendship with Benji wasn't a complete surprise. It was in her nature to make friends. But it was unusual for her to have such a strong connection to one kid. That was enough thinking about Miles and his son, she decided, giving her pillow a firm punch. She needed her rest. Tomorrow she was taking Lilliana to the children's museum and she needed to be as alert as possible.

Luckily, once she'd become a mother, Jillian had perfected the art of falling asleep at a moment's notice. Sleep had become a valuable commodity that was rarer than she'd realized before Lilliana came along. She closed her eyes and willed herself to sleep.

"Wake now."

Jillian could swear that she'd only just dozed off, but Lilliana's insistent voice had her opening her eyes. The sun was streaming through the window, proof that daytime had arrived. Lilliana was standing in her crib, shaking the rail. When she realized Jillian was awake, she grinned and began to chant. "Out. Out."

"All right, boss lady baby," Jillian said. She threw off the warm blankets and crossed the room. Lilliana held up her arms and Jillian scooped her daughter into her embrace. Lilliana giggled and then pressed a sloppy kiss on Jillian's cheek. Jillian held her daughter close for a long moment, savoring the feel of her little girl in her arms. Lilliana was growing so fast, and Jillian knew that the time would come when Lilliana would resist these affectionate mother-daughter moments.

As if reading Jillian's mind, Lilliana strained against the embrace. "Down."

"How about a dry diaper first?" Jillian suggested. Without waiting for a response, she set Lilliana back into her crib and did a quick diaper change before standing her on the floor.

Lilliana instantly scampered to the door. Jillian

grabbed her hand and they walked down the stairs together and to the kitchen. After a quick breakfast, Jillian got herself and Lilliana dressed in matching sweaters and jeans and then went into the living room.

"We're going to the children's museum," Jillian said to her parents.

"Is that right?" her mother asked from her seat on the sofa. She and Jillian's father were enjoying their morning coffee together.

"Yes. I think Lilliana would enjoy herself. And I wouldn't mind getting a look around town."

"There have been a few changes," her father said. "There's a new interior design business and a few more boutiques." He smiled at Jillian's mother as he said that. Valerie loved her fashion. "And a couple of new families have settled in town. Even so, Aspen Creek still has that familiar, welcoming feel."

"I've noticed that. I met a few new people at playgroup. But I'm looking forward to attending more events. I want Lilliana to grow up the way I did. I want her to make good friends and create wonderful memories."

"It sounds like she has," Valerie said. "According to Michelle, Lilliana and Benji are as thick as thieves. She says that Benji talks about his Lily all the time."

"They have played together at playgroup," Jillian admitted. "But they've only met a couple of times."

"Sometimes people just click. You know that. You and Miles were the very same way as kids. Once the two of you became friends, that was it. You wouldn't go anywhere without him. You made sure that Miles was included in everything from birthday parties to movies to bonfires. If you went, he went."

Jillian shrugged, not wanting to discuss her past relationship with Miles. It was still too complicated and her emotions, too confusing. Even so, her mind immediately returned to last night. It had felt so wonderful to be in his arms again, inhaling his familiar scent. She couldn't recall the last time she'd felt as content.

But no matter how right it felt, she knew he wasn't right for her. They would never work together. And no amount of wishing would change that.

"Well, Miles has friends of his own now."

"That's a good thing, right?" Henry asked.

"Absolutely. And I'm sure Benji will do the same." Jillian dressed Lilliana in her snowsuit and pulled her boots over her gym shoes. She put on her own coat and then kissed her parents goodbye. "See you later."

As they drove to downtown Aspen Creek, Jillian pointed out the scenery to her daughter. Although they came this way for playgroup, Jillian knew that it was going to take seeing the landmarks many times before it all became familiar to Lilliana. Jillian wanted Lilliana to feel at home. Of course, Lilliana felt at home wherever Jillian was.

Jillian found a parking spot on a side street across from the children's museum. When they stepped inside, laughter greeted them. Lilliana turned toward the sound. "Lily play?"

"That's right. We're going to go play with the kids."

"Enji?"

Jillian closed her eyes. Perhaps her parents were right. Clearly Lilliana associated Benji with fun.

"I don't know. Benji might be with his daddy today. It might just be the two of us, ladybug." She kissed Lilliana's plump cheek, making her laugh gustily.

Jillian removed their coats and Lilliana's boots, secured them in a locker and slipped the elastic keychain around her wrist. There was so much to see, and for a moment she and Lilliana just took in everything, looking first to the left and then to the right. A woman was seated at a table in the corner, doing face painting, a line of wiggling children waiting for their turns. Straight ahead was a small petting zoo with baby goats, pigs and lambs, which had been advertised as the special activity for this week. Three teenagers were instructing the kids who were surrounding them on the proper way to play with the animals. There were interactive scientific exhibits off to the right and upstairs on the second floor. And a large part of the first floor was taken up with a kiddy train station connected to tracks that ran throughout the room. Lilliana started in that direction.

"Well, that was easy," Jillian said to herself. When they reached the queue, Lilliana headed for the front of the line. "Oh, no, we have to wait our turn."

"Wait?" Lilliana's voice contained a hint of disappointment, but she took her place in line. She spun in a circle and then her eyes lit up and she squealed. "Enji."

Lilliana started to run off and Jillian reached out and grabbed her before she could get too far. Jillian spotted Miles and her heart began to race. Why was that still happening to her? She knew it was irrational, but she was suddenly irritated with Miles for being so darn attractive. A frown threatened and she forced it away. She'd agreed to be friends with him and she always kept her word. Besides, she didn't want Benji to think she was unhappy to see him. She liked him quite a bit. It was his father who made her want to run into the hills and hide.

Miles and Benji had spotted them and flashed identical smiles. Benji ran in their direction, Miles close on his heels. As they drew nearer, Lilliana clapped her hands and danced a happy jig.

Benji and Lilliana hugged as if they hadn't seen each other in ages. The joy between them was palpable and Jillian's heart warmed at the sight. In that moment she knew it would be wrong to come between them simply because being around Miles was difficult for her. Their friendship was just as important to them as Jillian's friendships were to her.

"Hi," Miles said. His voice was warm, and he seemed completely at ease, as if their previous encounters hadn't been uncomfortable.

"Hi. I didn't expect to see you here." Jillian cringed internally. What an inane thing to say.

"Benji isn't a fan of crowds, but he likes to play on the minibus and in the water exhibits. I figured we'd come early and be gone before it gets too crowded. Not that Aspen Creek is a bustling metropolis."

She nodded and there was a long silence between them. Jillian glanced at the kids. Benji had pulled a toy horse from his pocket and was showing it to Lilliana, who was suitably impressed. Their heads were so close together that they nearly touched. Once Jillian and Miles had been that close.

And then he'd broken her heart.

Miles leaned closer, his familiar scent wafting around her, teasing her senses and weakening her knees. "I had a great time with you last night. That's the most fun I've had in years."

"That was a one-time thing so don't get used to it." She was talking to herself as well as to him and her voice came out more sharply than she'd intended. He didn't seem to notice.

"I don't go out all that much, so there's no danger of that."

"Same."

"But after last night, staying in every night has lost its appeal. I think it was a mistake to isolate myself." He glanced at his son, the love in his eyes unmistakable. "Don't get me wrong, I love my son. After the divorce, I put all of my energy into Benji, trying to give him the love of two people. I didn't want him to think he'd done something to make his mother leave. I told him we were a crew of two. Now I wonder if that was a mistake. I wonder if we should expand our team."

"So what? You're looking to get married again?" She didn't know why that thought disturbed her as much as it did, but even saying the words made her heart hurt. She hoped it wasn't a sign that some part of her heart was still pining for him. That would be foolish and she'd only end up hurt again.

"No. Not at all," Miles said, and Jillian's heart began to beat normally again. "Benji and I aren't ready for such a drastic change in our lives. But it will do us both some good if I get out more. I want Benji to see me enjoying my life so he'll enjoy his. To be honest, we haven't been going to playgroup very long. At first, he didn't seem to like it and he put up a fuss about going. He wouldn't play at all unless I played with him. And he cried when I left the room with the other parents."

Jillian's heart filled with sympathy for the tyke. Although Lilliana had never been shy or clingy, Jillian empathized with Miles. It had to be painful to watch your child struggle and be helpless to change the situation.

"He seems to like it now," Jillian said.

"Maybe. Or it could be that he likes Lilliana. She's the only kid that he's played with on his own since we started going."

"She does have that effect on people. I don't think a kid has been born that Lilliana hasn't connected with. She's just that kind of person, you know?"

He grinned at her. "I'm familiar with the type."

His eyes twinkled with mischief and, despite telling herself to break the connection, she couldn't look away from his gaze. It was as if his deep, dark eyes had the power to hypnotize her, leaving her powerless to resist. The ridiculous thought shocked her out of her trance.

"It's our turn," she said, grateful to be able to look away from Miles without making her struggle obvious.

The teenager in charge of the ride smiled at Benji and Lilliana. "Are you ready to ride the train?"

"Twain!" Lilliana exclaimed and Benji nodded.

"Let's get you on then." He looked at Miles and

Jillian. "Two kids can fit in the bench seat, so we'll strap them in together."

Lilliana didn't hesitate. She let the youth take her hand and help her into the car. The open train was painted in bright colors and Jillian immediately took out her phone and took a picture of Lilliana, who was holding out a hand. "Enji. Come."

Benji looked up at Miles, who smiled encouragingly. "I'll be right here waiting for you."

"You aren't coming?"

"I'm too big."

Benji hesitated.

"Benji, I would love to take your picture with Lilliana. Do you think you can get in next to her?" Jillian asked. She smiled her brightest smile. Benji looked from her and then to Lilliana, who was now patting the empty seat beside her. He nodded and sat down.

A few moments later, the train pulled off. The track ran in a circle along the first floor of the museum, passing other exhibits designed to entice young minds, so it would return in about ten minutes. It moved slowly and Jillian and Miles could actually walk beside the car carrying Lilliana and Benji if they chose.

"Do you want to follow them?" Miles asked.

"No. We can see them from here. They'll be fine."

"I know."

"But?"

"I don't want Benji to panic if he can't see me."

Jillian compressed her lips, holding back her comment. After all, Benji was Miles's child, not hers. She wouldn't appreciate unsolicited advice on how to raise her daughter. It wasn't as if they were close friends.

"What?" Miles said.

"*What* what?"

"I know you, Jillian. You want to say something, but you're holding back."

"That's because it's none of my business."

He rubbed a hand over his face, clearly aggravated. He blew out a breath. "Just say it."

"All right. But remember, you asked."

He waved a hand. "Yeah, yeah. Just spit it out. Hearing what you have to say has to be better than watching you gnaw on your bottom lip."

"I think you're overprotective of Benji."

He frowned. "You sound like my mother."

"I don't want to nag."

"You aren't. And neither is she." He closed his eyes briefly. When he opened them, she saw the sorrow there. The worry. "It's just that Benji has changed so much since his mother left."

"How often does she see him?"

"As often as she can, but not as much as I'd like. But she calls him every week and sends him gifts all the time. To be honest, she wasn't ready for motherhood, but she's trying her best. I can't ask for more than that."

"This doesn't make sense. But then, who am I to judge? My ex has very little contact with Lilliana. He pays regular child support, but he hasn't seen her at all since he left. I want Lilliana to have a relationship with him, but I can't force it. All I can do is leave the door open for him while protecting my child in the best way I know how."

He blew out a breath. "I just want so much more for my son. And despite everything, I had expected better from Rachel."

Jillian could relate to that and she was upset on his and Benji's behalf. There was so much Jillian could say about the other woman, but she stopped herself. Her ranting wouldn't change a thing. At the end of the day, for all intents and purposes, Benji would still be a motherless child. Clearly neither she nor Miles had picked the best parents for their kids.

"I'm sorry that happened to Benji," Jillian settled for saying. "And I can understand the need to make up for the loss of his mother's love. I'm just as guilty when it comes to Lilliana and her father. From what I can see, you're a great dad. Helping him trust that you'll be waiting for him will go a long way to helping him come out of his shell."

"So running across the building and chasing the train is out."

A dimple flashed in his cheek, and she laughed.

That was one thing she always admired about Miles. He was good-natured about taking criticism, rarely getting offended.

"Not if you're trying to convince Benji you'll always be there for him, because the train is pulling into the station now."

They turned and watched as the train came into view. Benji and Lilliana were seated in the third car and Miles and Jillian waited patiently for the teenager to help the children get out. Lilliana and Benji were smiling from ear to ear and Jillian nudged Miles in the side. "I told you he'd be okay."

"That was fun," Benji said, grinning up at Miles.

"I bet."

"Can we do it again?"

Miles pointed at the line of children waiting for their turn. "Maybe later, bud. There are some other kids who want a turn."

"Okay. What are we going to do now?"

Miles glanced at Jillian. Jillian and Lilliana could go off on their own, but it was always more fun with a friend. Truth be told, Jillian was having as much fun with Miles as Lilliana was with Benji. There was no reason they shouldn't keep enjoying themselves. And that was one way to ensure that Benji and Miles didn't cling to each other too tightly. With Lilliana by his side, Benji would definitely be drawn into the fray because she wouldn't have it any other way.

"How about the petting zoo?" Jillian suggested. "Or would that be too boring for Benji? After all, you guys live on a ranch. Animals might not be a big deal to him."

"We live on a cattle ranch," Miles corrected. "The animals are big and dangerous, so he isn't allowed to be around them. He'll enjoy the petting zoo."

"I like pigs," Benji said.

Lilliana's experience with animals had been limited to the geriatric dog owned by one of their neighbors in Kansas. Bear had spent most of the time sleeping in the shade of an old oak tree. Even so, her smile widened as she echoed Benji's words, even though Jillian was sure she had no idea what a pig was.

Benji grabbed Lilliana's hand and then looked up at Miles. "We want to see the pigs."

"This way," Miles said as he took a step in the direction of the petting zoo.

As they headed over to the animals, Benji pointed out things that might interest Lilliana, once detouring to show her the fountain in the center of the building. Lilliana clapped her hands in glee as the water shot into the air. Benji beamed with pride and puffed out his small chest. Clearly Lilliana was good for his ego.

The line for the petting zoo was short and within minutes they were listening as the volunteer explained how to pet the pig without hurting it. Once again Jillian pulled out her phone and snapped photos of Lilliana and Benji. When they'd had their fill of the pig, they moved on to the baby goats.

"Aren't you going to take pictures of Benji?" Jillian asked Miles, who'd only been watching the interaction.

"Oh. I didn't even think of it." He fumbled in his pocket and pulled out his phone.

"Don't worry about it. I'll text you my photos."

"You'll need my number for that." His grin was so mischievous that for a moment his air of parental worry disappeared. Since she knew she also had that same air, she could understand it. Becoming a parent came with concerns she hadn't anticipated. But she had to admit the slightly more carefree Miles was attractive.

"So I will." She found herself grinning. "Are you going to give me your number or am I going to have to guess?"

He shook his head. "You already have it. Or you should unless you deleted it. I never changed it."

"You still have the same number?"

He nodded.

She didn't know what to make of that. Once she'd accepted that things were over between them, she'd changed her number. Not because she was worried that he might call her. But because she knew he wouldn't. Her heart couldn't bear further proof of his rejection.

"I think I still know it." She dialed his number, and his phone rang.

"Yep. That's me."

"Good. Now you have my number, too."

Something that resembled disappointment flashed in his eyes. He blinked and it vanished so fast she might have imagined it. There was no reason he should be disappointed that she'd changed her number. People did it all the time for a variety of reasons. Yet somehow he seemed to know that he'd been the catalyst for this change.

"Thanks." He typed on his phone screen, adding her name and number to his contacts. While he did that, she texted him copies of the pictures she'd taken and then turned her attention back to the little ones. And just in time. They were on the verge of becoming bored with the animals.

"How about we get some popcorn and hot chocolate?" Jillian suggested.

"Yay!" Benji clapped his hands and Lilliana did the same. Jillian quickly took wipes and hand sanitizer from her purse and cleaned their hands. When she was satisfied with the results, they walked to the concession stand. As they went, they passed numerous people who smiled at them. No doubt, the four of them once again looked like a happy family, this time enjoying a Sunday afternoon outing.

And had it not been for Miles, they actually could have been. Jillian frowned at the thought.

"Uh-oh. What's wrong?" Miles asked.

"What do you mean?"

"The look on your face says that something is wrong. I would have heard if someone said something to upset you. And I didn't hear a thing. Which could only mean that you just had a negative thought. Care to share?"

"Not really."

"It might make you feel better."

"I highly doubt it."

"Which can only mean one thing. I'm somehow involved in this thought."

"How do you do that?"

"Know what you're thinking?"

She nodded.

"Well, I don't know exactly what you're thinking. That's why I asked. But I can tell that something is wrong because I've known you since we were Benji and Lilliana's age."

"But we haven't been friends in years. Until I moved back, we hadn't spoken in the longest time."

"Maybe. But despite everything that has happened between us, our basic natures haven't changed. Our reactions and expressions are still the same. Our connection might not be as strong, but it's there."

She blew out a breath, unwilling to go that far.

There was no way they still shared a connection. He'd broken it years ago.

"So go on and tell me what has dimmed the light of your smile, Jillian, so that we can get back to enjoying our day."

"You're assuming that after I say what's on my mind things will get better instead of worse."

"I'm willing to take my chances."

"Okay." She took a deep breath and then, after checking to make sure that the kids were occupied – they were looking at a quarter Benji had found on the floor, she blurted, "I was thinking that we look like a family and that we could have been. If not for you."

Chapter Seven

"*If not for me.*" His voice was flat. Devoid of any emotion.

She nodded. "Yeah. Everything was perfect be-tween us. We had a great life. I thought we were going to have a wonderful future."

"Until I wanted to take a break."

"You ended things between us."

"To be sure that we were together for the right reason. Because we belonged together, and weren't just with each other out of habit."

"Because you thought you might be missing out on something better than me."

"That wasn't it at all. I just wasn't sure. And I wanted to be sure."

He'd said that before. At the time, she hadn't

wanted to hear it. Truthfully, she wasn't that thrilled about hearing it now. The difference was, she wasn't operating on pain today. Even in the short amount of time that had passed since she'd come back to Aspen Creek, she'd begun to see things differently. The hurt that she'd experienced the first time she'd seen him had faded and diminished, leaving her able to view the past more clearly.

"I understand that now," she said.

"Good. So can we put the past in the past and leave it there?"

She nodded. "I'll try. It's not that easy." He raised an eyebrow and she sighed. "Okay. The past is over and done."

"Good. Let's get our snack and grab a table."

They bought boxes of buttered popcorn and mugs of hot chocolate.

When it was time to pay, Benji held out his quarter. "I have money."

"I'll pay this time," Miles said. "Put the quarter in your pocket and we'll put it in your bank when we get home."

"Okay."

They found a table for four off the beaten path. The kids had declared they also wanted hot dogs, so they'd gotten those, as well. Once they were seated, Jillian opened the condiment packets and squirted mustard on Lilliana's bun. Miles grabbed a ketchup packet and reached for Benji's hot dog, but his son held it away.

"I want Jilly to put it on."

"Oh."

Jillian heard the uncertainty in Miles's voice over his son's rejection. She was surprised by Benji's request herself but decided not to make a big deal of it. "Of course, Benji."

She squirted on the ketchup and a bit of relish and then handed his hot dog back to him.

"Thank you," Benji said, smiling.

"You're welcome," Jillian replied before whispering to Miles. "I hope that was okay."

Miles nodded. "If I want him to be less dependent on me, I have to get used to him turning to other people for help."

"That's the spirit."

"Besides, if not for Benji's attachment to you, I'm not sure we'd be sharing these delicacies."

"Delicacies? Your standards leave something to be desired. Not that I'm complaining. The hot dog is good and the company is…passable."

Miles threw back his head and laughed loudly. Jillian took the opportunity to look at him without him noticing. Dressed in black jeans and a gray sweatshirt advertising a local feed store, he looked too handsome for words.

She glanced down at herself. She was dressed in faded jeans and a pink sweater. She felt cute and knew that she was holding her own in the appearance department. Not that it mattered. Miles wasn't interested in her that way. For the first time ever, that thought didn't break her heart. Some people weren't destined to be lovers. Jillian and Miles were two of those people. But that didn't mean they couldn't be friends. Judging by how well they were getting along now, it was clear that she could handle having a purely platonic relationship with him. After all, they'd been friends long before they'd become lovers.

"Passable company? Well, then, I'm luckier than you are because I'm graced with wonderful company."

He smiled and her heart lurched. *Friends, Jillian.* That's all they were going to be. Hopefully she wouldn't have to remind herself of that fact every time they were together.

Lilliana reached out for her cup. Jillian helped her daughter sip her drink, taking the moment to slow her galloping heart. When Lilliana had drunk her fill, Jillian turned back to Miles.

"I don't suppose you would want to get them together in the future?"

"You mean for a playdate?" Jillian asked.

He shook his head. "When did they start calling it that? I remember when kids used to go to their friend's house to play and that was it. We didn't need a fancy name for it."

"When did you turn into a grumpy grandpa?"

"It just seems a bit ridiculous to me. But whatever. Do you want to bring Lilliana over to play one day next week?"

She nodded. "Yes."

When they finished eating, Benji looked at Miles. "Can we ride the train now?"

Miles glanced at Jillian and she shrugged. It didn't matter to her. The whole idea was for the kids to have a good time. If riding the train was what they wanted to do, it was okay with her. "Do you want to ride the train, Lilliana?"

Lilliana nodded. "Twain wif Enji."

"Well, I guess we have our answer," Jillian said. They gathered their trash and then placed it in the nearest can before returning to the kiddy train depot.

There was only a short line so within minutes the kids were once more seated in the train. This time, Benji didn't have to be coaxed into the car, but rather stepped right onto it, a proud grin on his face. When the train pulled away, Benji and Lilliana waved and then began chatting to each other.

"I guess you were right," Miles said.

"Naturally. Did you doubt it?" Jillian laughed. "But would you mind telling me about what specifically?"

"About not following the train while Benji rode it. He was so confident this time. I doubt he would have behaved the same way if I had walked beside him the entire way."

"It's hard to watch them grow up."

"You seem to have mastered it."

Jillian laughed. "Don't be deceived. It's hard for me, too. It's just that Lilliana is such an independent child. I swear she has never let me baby her."

He laughed. "The more I hear about her, the more like you she sounds."

"Which is good and bad at the same time."

"You said it, not me." He paused. "Benji has never been a bold child, but he wasn't always this clingy. Rachel's leaving really knocked him for a loop and he hasn't bounced back yet."

"He will. You're a great dad. Give it time."

"Time. How much time?" His mouth turned down. She sensed the helplessness that surrounded him.

He looked so miserable that, before Jillian could think it through, she reached out and hugged him. The moment her arms went around his neck, her heart sped up and the blood began racing through her veins. The heat from his body wrapped around her, at once soothing and arousing. She was in dangerous territory. Before she could tell herself to step back, his arms encircled her, and he pulled her closer. She inhaled his tantalizing and familiar scent. His muscular chest was hard against her breasts. The years fell away and in that brief moment, they were as they'd once been. She'd intended the embrace to offer comfort, but that was no longer the case. Now she was filled with yearning. Desire. If she stayed in Miles's arms any longer, those emotions would get the best of her. That would be catastrophic for her and their burgeoning friendship.

Slowly Jillian eased back.

The train returned, saving her from making a fool of herself and giving her the opportunity to move away from Miles.

The children had been talking together happily, but they'd ended their conversation and were now tugging on their parents' arms to get their attention.

"Sorry, bud," Miles said to Benji. "What do you need?"

Benji shrugged, unable to put his feelings into words. This wasn't unusual, so Miles did what he always did. He stooped down and then pulled Benji into his arms for a hug. Benji leaned into him and sighed deeply. He needed attention and affection now, the assurance that his dad was there. Because even though he hadn't had a problem getting onto the train, he had been separated from Miles long enough for doubts and fears to creep in.

As Miles stood to his full height, he tossed Benji into the air and then placed him onto his shoulders. Benji laughed and kicked his feet a couple of times, striking Miles in the chest. One of these days he was going to remember to hold onto Benji's feet so that he didn't end up with tyke-sized cowboy boot bruises.

Lilliana looked up and clapped and laughed. Then she reached out her hands, stretching her arms and standing on her tiptoes. "Me. Me. Up."

Miles glanced at Jillian, who nodded, so Miles leaned up and caught Benji's eyes. "Lilliana wants me to pick her up now. Is that okay with you? Can she have a turn?"

Benji nodded. "Lily is my friend."

Miles lowered Benji from his shoulders, taking a moment to hug him before setting him on the ground.

"Are you ready, Lilliana?"

Lilliana nodded and clapped her hands in anticipation. Before he could reach her, she jumped up in what he supposed was her attempt to hasten the process.

"Up now," she demanded.

"Yes, ma'am."

He stooped down and very carefully lifted her into his arms. It was one thing to toss his son into the air and catch him before setting him on his shoulders. It was another to treat a delicate little girl with the same abandon. When he settled her onto his shoulders, she squealed and laughed loudly. "Enji. Look."

Benji nodded at her, his smile happy, clearly not

the least bit jealous of the attention Miles was show-ing Lilliana.

Miles looked from Benji to Jillian, who had a wistful smile on her face. It wasn't hard to guess her mood. She was thinking of all that her daughter missed by not having a father active in her life. He felt the same way about Benji not having his mother around.

After a few minutes, he lowered Lilliana to the ground, making sure that she was steady on her feet before he stepped away. Before he could move, Lilliana grabbed him by the neck and kissed his cheek. His heart melted at the affectionate gesture, and he needed to swallow several times to clear the lump that materialized in his throat.

He stood and then looked at the trio. Benji was holding Jillian's right hand and Lilliana had her left. Miles was struck by the notion that they belonged together. That Jillian had been right. If not for him, they would have been a family. But he also had to face the sad truth that their time had passed. There was no going back to the way things had been. He'd just been thinking how grateful he was to have Jillian back in his life. He wasn't going to get greedy for more or do anything to jeopardize their burgeoning friendship.

Lilliana yawned and rubbed her eyes. Jillian grinned. "It looks like someone is getting sleepy.

It's time to get this little one home for her nap before she starts getting cranky."

"That sweetie? I can't imagine her being anything other than a ray of sunshine."

"Most of the time she is. But when she's hungry or sleepy? That ray of sunshine turns into a thunderstorm really quickly."

Miles couldn't help but laugh. That description could also describe the Jillian of his youth. She'd been popular because she'd been fun, sweet and adventurous. But if she saw an injustice or thought someone was being mistreated? *Whew.* Volcanoes had nothing on her when she blew her top. "Like someone I know."

"You sound like Marty. He swears that Lilliana acts just like I did when we were kids. Of course, I was following him around and we were getting into so much trouble together that he can't claim innocence now." Lilliana yawned again and held up her arms, so Jillian picked up her daughter. "That's my sign. I'll see you later. Bye, Benji. See you soon."

"Bye, Jilly. Bye Lily."

Lilliana's eyes were drifting shut, but she managed to waggle her fingers in a reasonable facsimile of a wave. Benji must have found it acceptable because he smiled and slid his hand into Miles's. They stood side by side, watching as Jillian and Lilliana left, not looking away until they were out of sight. Miles heard Benji sigh and he seconded that emotion with a sigh of his own. The light and fun of the day had faded. Jillian and Lilliana had taken it with them.

"Do you want to ride the train again?" Miles asked.

Benji shook his head.

"Do you want to go to the petting zoo again? Or maybe get your face painted?"

"No."

"Then what do you want to do?"

"Go home."

"You sure?"

He nodded. "Lily and Jilly left."

Before they'd seen Jillian and Lilliana, Benji had been content to spend the day with Miles. But that was before he'd experienced the fun and excitement that Jillian and Lilliana had brought with them. Suddenly being a crew of two wasn't all that great.

"That sounds like a plan."

Miles told himself that he wasn't disappointed by the turn of events, but that was only partially true. Although he wished Jillian and Lilliana would have stayed longer, he suddenly felt like he wasn't enough. Benji grinned sheepishly and held up his free arm. "Carry me, Daddy."

"Sure, bud." He swung Benji over his head and set him on his shoulders. Benji laughed and pointed at different things as they walked through the museum, stopping to buy a cotton candy for the road.

Benji insisted on sharing the way too sweet confection with Miles, but he managed to choke it down as they left the museum and crossed the street to his truck. Once they were inside, Miles started the forty-five-minute drive back to the ranch.

By the time they passed the Aspen Creek mall, Benji had fallen asleep, the paper cone of his cotton candy clutched securely in his hand. His head was tilted to the side, and he was drooling. Miles's heart filled with love as he looked at his son.

Miles pulled up to his house and parked. He considered waking Benji but decided against it. After placing his son in his bed for a nap, Miles went back outside and stared over the valley. His family ranch was a good size. The majority of the land was devoted to grazing, but there were many scenic spots. Miles had chosen one of his favorite locations to build his house. He had an outstanding view of nature from every window, but his favorite scene was visible from his back deck. He had a clear view of the hills that led to a winding stream. And of course, the Rockies in the distance.

There was something soothing about the mountains. No matter how bad his day, looking at them cleared his head and gave him a different perspective. His problem didn't go away, but the mountains often put him in a better frame of mind to deal with it and come up with a workable solution. Now, though, as he stared at the mountains, he didn't see the snowcapped peaks, or the soaring trees reaching for the clear blue sky. Instead, he saw Jillian's brilliant smile.

"How was the museum?" Valerie asked when Jillian stepped into the house.

"It was wonderful." Jillian toed off her snow boots and then set them on the mat near the door to dry.

"What about you, Lilliana?" Henry asked. "Did you have fun?"

Lilliana smiled at her grandfather. She toddled over and gave him a big hug. "Juice?"

Henry glanced at Jillian. "A little orange juice would be fine."

"Cookie?"

"Just one, please," Jillian said.

"Of course." Henry took Lilliana's hand and the two of them headed for the kitchen.

"Grandparents prerogative," Valerie said.

"I didn't say a word."

"So, the museum was fun."

"Yes. I ran into Miles."

"Really?"

"He and Benji had the same idea we had. We actually hung out together the entire time. It was nice. More than nice. It was fun."

"I'm glad to hear it. So does this mean that your broken heart is finally mended?"

Jillian was silent for a moment, checking in with her feelings. She pictured Miles and there wasn't even the slightest pang. Quite the opposite. She felt happy. She realized that they'd begun to slip into a comfortable relationship. They weren't as close as they'd once been, and she wasn't sure she'd call them friends yet, but they were more than acquaintances. Better than that, they weren't enemies.

"Yes. It has taken a while, but I'm no longer in pain. I guess time really does heal all ills."

"That's wonderful. Now you're able to head into the future with optimism instead of a sense of dread."

"I know. I just need to figure out what the future holds."

"It holds whatever you want it to hold. The possibilities are endless. There are career opportunities as well as future romantic interests."

Jillian made the time-out signal with her hands. "Hold on there, Mom. I might not still be holding a grudge against Miles, but the ink is barely dry on my divorce. Surely you aren't suggesting that I start dating again."

Valerie leaned forward in her chair, an indication that she was about to say something serious. Jillian's stomach tightened nervously. Even though she knew whatever her mother said would be spoken out of love, Jillian wasn't sure she was ready for a deep conversation right now. But since there was no way to stop Valerie from speaking her mind, Jillian listened.

"The time since your divorce doesn't matter. To be honest, I know you were disappointed when things with Evan didn't work out, but I don't believe you were heartbroken. At least not to the same extent you were when Miles ended things between you. Am I wrong?"

Jillian shook her head. "No, you're right."

"I never thought Evan was right for you. I think you turned to him on the rebound. I wasn't entirely surprised that things didn't work out."

"Do you think I'm the reason Evan left us? Because I didn't love him enough?"

"That's not what I said. He's responsible for his own actions. Hopefully he'll realize what he's missing out on by not being a part of his daughter's life and change his behavior."

"I hope so, too. I know I made it more difficult for him when I left Kansas, but I needed to come home."

"He'll figure it out and do what's necessary. But you're missing my point entirely."

"Sorry. I just feel guilty about how things turned out for Lilliana."

"Get used to it. A mother's guilt knows no bounds." Valerie said the words with a smile, but they struck a nerve. "If it helps, I think you're doing all the right things. You're a wonderful mother."

Jillian's throat tightened and she could only whisper, "Thank you."

"Now. Back to my point. The reason you're ready for love again has nothing to do with Evan. He didn't break your heart. Rather it has everything to do with Miles."

"Miles? We were over years ago. It just took me a while to accept it."

"And now that you have there's nothing stopping you from opening your heart to someone else."

Jillian laughed. "What about Lilliana? Shouldn't I be focused on her instead of worrying about romance?"

"Why do you have to choose? You can still be a great mother without giving up on love. If things had worked with Evan, you would have still been a mother and had a romantic relationship. So why not now?"

Jillian couldn't think of a good reason why not. Except, despite her brave words about her feelings for Miles being dead, a part of her knew with the right incentive they could easily be resuscitated. Knowing that, it would be foolish to enter into another relationship until she was sure she was completely over Miles.

But how would she know? More importantly, how long would it take?

Chapter Eight

"Well, someone's in a good mood."

Miles paused in the process of saddling his horse, turning at the sound of Isaac's voice. As always, his younger brother was smiling. Miles grinned in return. "I'm always in a good mood."

Aaron, the ranch hand Nathan had hired a few months ago choked out a laugh. As Aaron was one of the most taciturn people Miles had ever met, the laughter was a surprise. Miles glanced at Aaron who shrugged and swung onto his saddle and rode out of the stable.

"Well let's just say you're in a better mood than you've been in the past. I wonder at the cause. Could it be Jilly?"

"Since when do you call her that?" Miles asked.

"That's what my nephew calls her. I stopped by the main house before I came out here. He was telling Mom all about riding the train with Lily and eating lunch with Jilly."

Miles shook his head. Those two had become Benji's favorite topic of conversation these days. His quiet son was full of observations about Jillian and Lilliana.

"We ran into them at the children's museum. He and Lilliana like each other so we hung out together. What's wrong with that?" Miles realized he was sounding defensive and told himself to dial it back.

Isaac mounted his horse and stared at Miles. "Who said anything was wrong with it? Just let me know if I need to get my tux cleaned."

"Wait a minute," Miles said. But it was too late. Isaac had already ridden away. "Nobody is thinking about getting married," Miles said to the empty building.

He jumped onto his horse and then rode after his brother and Aaron. They were moving the cattle from one field to another today. It would take most of the day, but Miles didn't mind. This was actually one of his favorite jobs on the ranch. He loved being on horseback and didn't mind when one of the cows tried to make a break for it.

The sun was shining in the clear blue sky, but it did little to warm up the day. Once they got moving, he would warm up. He blew on his gloved hands. "Let's go."

Thor and Loki, the two border collies they used to herd cattle jumped to their feet and raced over to Miles.

He didn't wait for Aaron or Isaac to reply before kicking his horse into a gallop across the field. The ground was frozen, and patches of brown grass occasionally peaked out beneath the ice and snow.

The horses' hooves thundered as they covered the ground, steam blowing from their nostrils. After about twenty minutes, they reached the north field where the cattle were currently grazing.

The dogs immediately began walking around, waiting for the order to go.

"I'll ride up front," Aaron volunteered. "That way the two of you can talk."

He rode away before Miles or Isaac could reply. "That's the most I've ever heard him say," Isaac said. "He's probably wants to be alone to recover from the overstimulation."

"Not everyone feels the need to fill every silence," Miles said.

"Maybe not, but you have to admit that he's a bit secretive."

"Maybe he likes his privacy. And since I hated being gossiped about, I'm not to speculate about him."

"Fine. I'd much rather talk about you and Jillian anyway."

Miles rolled his eyes and turned his horse away. He signaled Aaron to start moving the cattle, hoping that Isaac would take the hint. He should have known better.

"So, are you dating?"

"We're friends."

"That's an improvement from before."

Miles couldn't help but smile and felt his general reticence fade away. Isaac might be annoying, but he could be trusted to keep a secret. "She's coming over for a playdate."

"Oh. You're taking a page out of my book."

"I should have said she's bringing her daughter to play with Benji, but I figured that was understood."

"There's nothing that says you can't play, too."

"For the last time, we don't have that type of relationship."

"Make that move and maybe you will."

Miles shook his head. He recalled how Jillian had pulled away from him after she'd hugged him at the children's museum. She'd been uncomfortable with the physical contact. They hadn't seen each other since then, so he doubted that. "There's no move to be made. Our romantic relationship ended years ago. I'm happy just to have her friendship."

"If you say so," Isaac said and then rode away before Miles could reply. But then, there was nothing left to say. Miles wasn't going to do anything to ruin his new friendship with Jillian.

* * *

"Hold still so I can get you out of your seat," Jillian said. Lilliana giggled and kicked her legs a few more times. Jillian leaned against the open car door and waited for Lilliana's case of the wiggles to pass. "All right. We'll stay here, but Benji is waiting to play with you."

"Enji?" Lilliana looked around hopefully.

"That's right. Benji. But we can't see him until you sit still." Lilliana stopped kicking. Jillian quickly released her daughter from the car seat, lifted her and then stood her on the ground. Jillian held Lilliana's hand and looked around. Miles had always talked about building his own home on the family ranch. When they'd been dating, he'd often shown her places that he'd been considering. At the time, she'd believed that he was asking for her opinion because he'd planned for her to live there with him. Now she knew that hadn't been the case, especially since the spot he'd chosen wasn't among the ones she'd liked the most.

She had to admit that he'd chosen a beautiful location. But then, the entire ranch was scenic. With hills and rivers in one direction, and an unobstructed view of the mountains in another, he couldn't go wrong with any spot.

Her heart skipped a beat when she thought about seeing Miles again. She hadn't been sleeping well lately. Every time she closed her eyes, she pictured

Miles as he'd looked at the museum. He'd been the epitome of a handsome cowboy and it had taken every ounce of self-control for her to keep her cool and maintain her distance. She'd done that pretty well until she hadn't.

Every night since then, Jillian had relived the moment when they'd embraced, recalling how good it had felt to have his arms wrapped around her. She'd felt so secure. As if she'd found where she truly belonged. That thought had been disturbing, but she hadn't been able to shake it. She'd tried to tell herself that she'd imagined the feeling, but she'd know it was time to face the truth. She was determined to be honest with herself. That was the only way to avert disaster.

So, after days of denial, and nights of tossing and turning, she'd admitted to herself that she was still attracted to Miles. That would be her secret. Nothing good could ever come from sharing those feelings with him. They might be on their way to becoming friends again, but that didn't mean she couldn't keep secrets from him. Some things weren't meant to be shared.

"Enji?" Lilliana said, tugging on Jillian's hand, shaking her out of her reverie.

"Yes, Benji. Let's go." The sun was shining brightly in the cloudless blue sky, although it did little to heat the cold late January day. Several inches of snow had fallen over night and Lilliana grinned at the footprints she left with each step.

Jillian and Lilliana held hands as they walked up the front stairs and onto the massive front porch. Before she could ring the bell, the door swung open.

"Hi," Miles said, a warm smile on his face.

"Where's Enji?" Lilliana asked. Without waiting for an answer, she brushed past him and walked into the house.

"Sorry," Jillian said. "Lilliana has a tendency to make herself at home."

"Not to worry. She's welcome. I like that she feels comfortable enough to barge past me," Miles said, leading Jillian into the living room. There were a bunch of toys on the floor. Lilliana was already sitting among them, pushing a red car back and forth.

"Where *is* Benji?" Jillian asked.

"I'm right here," Benji said, coming to stand beside Lilliana. He was holding his coat in his hands.

Jillian glanced at Miles.

"I thought Lilliana would enjoy seeing the horses. After all, she seemed to get a kick out of the animals in the petting zoo."

"Horsy?" Lilliana said? "Enji horsy."

"That's right. She did seem to like his toy horse." Jillian looked at Miles. "That sounds like a good plan."

Benji insisted on putting on his coat by himself and that took a few minutes. Eventually he was ready and they trooped back out the front door. They put Lilliana's car seat in Miles's SUV and drove the short distance to the stables.

As they drove, Jillian took the opportunity to look at the scenery. The ranch, with its soaring trees, acres of hill currently covered by snow, and the Rockies visible in the background, truly was beautiful.

The kids giggled as they got out of the car. It was snowing lightly again, but it probably wouldn't last more than fifteen or so minutes.

When they stepped inside the building, Lilliana wrinkled her nose. Then she sneezed.

"I hope she isn't allergic. Or catching a cold," Miles said.

"I doubt it. It might be dust. If she sneezes more, then I'll worry."

Miles nodded and stooped in front of Lilliana. "Are you ready to meet the horses?"

Lilliana smiled and nodded. Then she slid her hand into Miles's hand and reached out her other for Benji. Benji took it and then grabbed Jillian's and the four of them walked up to the first stall.

Princess, a gentle mare walked over to the gate and leaned over. She neighed and Lilliana laughed and clapped her hand.

"She's saying hello," Miles said.

"Hi Horsy," Lilliana said. "Good horsy."

Miles picked her up so she could rub the Princess's mane. Lilliana giggled.

"Lily likes Princess," Benji said gleefully.

"Yes, she does," Jillian agreed.

"Has she ever been on a horse?" Miles asked.

Jillian shook her head. "I lived in a city, remember? There weren't a lot of horses around,"

"I'm not judging you," Miles said quickly.

"I know. I guess I'm a bit sensitive. Lilliana hasn't had the same opportunities we had as kids growing up here."

"Well, if it's okay with you, I'll take her for a ride around the corral."

"Me too?" Benji asked.

"Yep. You too."

"All right," Jillian agreed.

Miles saddled Princess and led her to the corral where he mounted her. Jillian picked up Lilliana and set her in front of Miles who wrapped a hand securely around her middle. Lilliana grinned broadly and clapped her hands.

Miles gently nudged the horse who began walking slowly on the snow-covered grass.

"Go!" Lilliana exclaimed, kicking her feet and moving her body. "Go, Horsy!"

"Naturally your daughter would want to go fast," Miles said with a laugh before urging Princess into a trot.

Were it anyone else, Jillian might be nervous

about her daughter riding on a horse, but she knew Lilliana was perfectly safe with Miles.

After a ten-minute ride, Miles returned with Lilliana. She poked out her bottom lip when Jillian lifted her from the horse's back. "It's Benji's turn to ride. Okay?"

"'Kay."

"I want to go fast, too," Benji said.

Miles's eyebrows raised for a second and then he smiled. "You got it, bud."

Jillian sat Benji in front of Miles and watched as father and son rode around the corral. Benji grinned proudly, sitting straight in the saddle.

"Enji go," Lilliana said.

"Yes. Benji's riding the horse like you did."

Jillian heard footsteps and turned around as Nathan came to stand beside her.

"Hey, Nathan."

"Hey. Is this your little girl?"

"Yep. Lilliana, this is Benji's uncle."

"Hi," Lilliana said, grinning.

"Hi," Nathan replied and then turned to look at Jillian. "It's good to see you back on the ranch."

"It feels good. There's something so warm that I missed."

Miles returned with Benji.

"Hi Uncle Nathan. Did you see me go fast?"

"I did. You're a real rancher now." He helped

Benji from the horse and set him on his feet. "Won't be long before you can help with the cattle."

Benji puffed out his chest and grinned.

Miles swung from the horse. "I didn't know you were around."

"I stopped by to grab some food."

"I thought Mom and Dad went to Denver for the weekend."

"She saved me a plate. You know, because I'm her favorite."

Jillian laughed.

Miles snorted. "Keep thinking that."

Miles began leading the horse into the stables and Nathan stepped in front of him. "If you and Jillian want to go for a ride, I can watch the kids."

"You?" Miles asked.

"Me. I can drive them back to your house while you guys ride around."

Jillian's first instinct was to say yes. She'd missed riding and the thought of spending time on horseback was thrilling. But she hesitated. She knew Lilliana would be perfectly safe under Nathan's care. That wasn't the issue. Did she trust herself to be alone with Miles? Would her foolish heart get the wrong idea if they spent time alone?

Nathan looked at Jillian and grinned. "You know you want to."

There was no sense in denying it. And really, what was the harm in one short ride? "I do."

"Then it's settled." He held out his hand to Miles. "I'll take your car and you can bring me mine when you're done. Just give me your keys."

Miles looked at Jillian and she smiled. He looked back at his brother. "Okay. I'll owe you."

"Not really. But if you want to pay me back you can go to the Chamber of Commerce meeting for me."

Miles frowned. "That's a steep price. But it's one I'm willing to pay."

"I'll be going, too," Jillian said to Miles before turning to Nathan. "We won't be long."

"Take your time. I can handle two little kids."

Chapter Nine

Miles and Jillian helped Nathan get the kids settled in Miles's SUV and then returned to the barn. Princess was a nice horse for the little ones, but he knew Jillian would prefer a more spirited mount. He helped her saddle Valkyrie and then saddled Blaze, his personal horse.

Jillian swung into the saddle as if a day hadn't passed since they'd last ridden together when in reality it had been years.

"Ready?"

"More than you can imagine."

"Then let's go."

They rode from the stable and onto the snow-covered grass. By unspoken agreement, they headed the way they had always ridden. Across the ranch and up the hills until they reached a field beside a ravine.

Once Miles was sure that Jillian's skill hadn't diminished, he gave Blaze free rein and the horse began racing across the snow. Jillian's laughter reached him as she urged Valkyrie to go faster.

When they reached the ravine, they slowed to a stop.

"That was fun. I had forgotten just how much I like riding. And after a day like today, I needed it."

"Rough day?"

"You don't know the half of it."

"Care to share?"

She gave him a long look before nodding. "I started back to work. Only part time. There wasn't one incident in particular that was a problem. Just little fires that needed to be put out. Reservations that needed to be changed. A lost kid that turned out to be a kid who wasn't ready to go home so he was hiding in the restaurant bathroom. A wife and mistress running into each other on the slopes. I was supposed to be working in special events, but when your parents own the resort, you go where you're needed."

"Admit it. You love it."

"I did. I love being a mother, but I enjoy working, too."

"And you're a great mother. Lilliana has to be the most confident child I've met."

"Thanks." She smiled at his words and his blood heated. She sighed. "I guess we'd better get back. We don't want to take advantage of Nathan?"

Miles laughed. "Who doesn't? He's so sure he can handle two kids. I say let him."

"You're wrong for that."

He only stared at her.

"Okay," she agreed with a grin. "Thirty more minutes and then we're going back."

The next half hour passed quickly, but it held more fun that Miles had had in forever. Jillian was just as adventurous and daring as she'd ever been. And he was just as willing to follow her into mischief as he'd ever been.

When they rode the horses into the stable, he was exhilarated. "We should do that again."

"I agree," Jillian said.

They removed the saddles and took care of the horses before hopping in Nathan's car and driving to Miles's house.

They stepped inside and looked around. Nathan looked as harried as Miles had ever seen him. Lilliana was sitting on the floor, ramming two cars together and laughing at the sound they made when they crashed.

"Where's Benji?" Miles asked as he took off his coat and hung it on the hook near the front door. Jillian did the same.

Nathan turned in a slow circle. "He was here a

minute ago. They were playing together for a while. Then he decided they needed more toys. He's been carrying down toys from his room for the past twenty minutes. When it looked like he was going to bring down every toy that he owned, I told him that he had enough for the two of them to play with. I was under the impression that he agreed."

"Apparently you were wrong."

"Apparently. He must be upstairs emptying his toy box."

Jillian laughed as she took a car from Lilliana's clenched fist. "Roll them. Okay. No more demolition derby. You're giving Uncle Nathan a headache."

"Thank you," Nathan said, rubbing his forehead. "Benji is very different when he's alone. He's quieter. Happy to color or watch a movie. But with Lilliana? She had an influence on him. He was a totally different kid." Nathan gave Jillian a sheepish look. "No offense."

"None taken. I know my daughter is a little dynamo."

"I have more toys," Benji said, entering the room, a plastic bat in one hand and a ball in the other. He was holding a stuffed clown under his chin.

Lilliana dropped the car she was holding and raced over to Benji. Miles got to his son first and caught the clown before it slid to the floor.

"Doll," Lilliana demanded of Miles, reaching for

the stuffed toy. Miles handed over the clown and Lilliana clutched it to her chest.

Benji dropped the bat and ball on the pile of toys and then raced for the stairs.

"Where are you going, bud?" Miles asked.

"I need to get the tee."

"I'll get it," Miles said. "You stay here."

"And on that note, I'll make my escape," Nathan said, getting wearily to his feet.

"So should I add you to my list of babysitters?" Jillian asked.

Nathan raised an eyebrow.

"So that's a no?"

Lilliana ran over and grabbed Nathan's legs. "Up Unca Nate. Horsy."

Nathan stooped down to Lilliana's level. "Uncle Nathan is too tired to give you another horsy ride now. Okay?"

"'Kay."

He put on his hat and coat, waved and left.

"I didn't think it was possible, but I think they humbled my brother," Miles said returning. He held the plastic tee under his arm.

"Shame on you for laughing," Jillian said. But she was smiling too.

Lilliana and Benji sat on the floor and rolled the ball between them.

While the kids were occupied, Jillian took a quick look around. The room was enormous with sunlight streaming through the nearly floor-to-ceiling windows. The masculine decor consisted of leather sofas and chairs and wooden end tables holding large lamps. The artwork was limited to framed photos of Benji. There was something familiar and comfortable about the room. It reminded her of Miles.

"Are you really going to let them play T-ball in here?" Although the room was spacious and the furniture appeared sturdy, there was always the risk of the kids knocking over a lamp.

"Not in here. But sometimes Benji and I play in the family room. I don't have a lot of furniture in there, so we don't have to worry about breaking anything. Just so you know, we also have a small basketball net in there, too. Although we love playing outside, when it's cold we can only spend so much time in the elements before we need to take a break to warm up. But that doesn't mean that Benji's ready to stop running around."

"I know what you mean. For the most part Lilliana is content to play with her dolls, but every once in a while she can be very boisterous. In the winter, our outside time is limited. I love skiing and snowboarding, but since I've become a parent, I've started to appreciate warmer months when we can stay outside longer."

"Me, too. Hence the indoor basketball and T-ball setup."

They sat in companionable silence as they watched the children play. Jillian marveled at how easygoing Benji was. Lilliana could be a little stinker sometimes, taking a toy from Benji because she wanted to play with it. The first couple of times it happened, Jillian told Lilliana to give it back. Benji said Lilliana could keep it and simply grabbed another toy.

Lilliana kept up a stream of chatter and the quieter Benji nodded or laughed when appropriate.

"Benji is such a good boy. He doesn't seem to mind that Lilliana has commandeered his stuffed clown. She has it on her lap even though she's not playing with it."

"I'm a bit surprised about that myself. Not that he's sharing. But that he's sharing his clown. Rachel gave that to him for his birthday. He sleeps with it and doesn't even like for me to touch it when I help him make up his bed. Clearly Lilliana is special."

"No doubt about it."

The conversation lagged for a moment, but the silence wasn't uncomfortable. "I really like what I've seen of your house."

"Thanks. It took a while to build, but I'm happy with the way it turned out."

"I don't remember this being one of the locations you were considering." Perhaps his ex-wife had preferred the views from this spot and he'd built here in order to satisfy her. Jillian bit back the jealousy that threatened. Any good husband would consider his wife's input when making such a big decision. Besides, Jillian was done living in the past. His life, his choice.

"It wasn't."

"What made you decide to build here?"

He was silent for a minute, his fingers steepled. She hadn't intended this to be a tough question. In her mind it had been the next natural question to ask. He cleared his throat.

"You don't have to answer," Jillian said. "I didn't mean to put you on the spot."

"I know. I'm just not sure how you'll take it."

"I don't see that it has anything to do with me. Unless you're going to tell me that I was too pushy back when you were looking for a place to build."

"That's not what I was going to say."

"Then what?" She released the breath she'd been holding but relief didn't follow. She couldn't imagine what he was going to say, but since he was having difficulty finding the right words, it probably wasn't something she wanted to hear.

"I chose this spot because I couldn't build a house for Rachel on a place that you'd chosen. It didn't seem right."

"Because she might be offended? I guess I can understand that. And this is a great location."

He shook his head. "That's not it at all. I couldn't let another woman live on one of *your* favorite locations. We might have broken up, but in my mind, they still belonged to you."

"Oh."

Miles heard the words coming out of his mouth, but he couldn't believe he'd actually said them. Since Jillian had replied, he knew he hadn't imagined it. What had made him spill his guts like that? He'd never told anyone why he'd decided to build his house here.

Over time, he'd begun to realize what he'd lost when he'd let Jillian walk out of his life. But by then it was too late. He'd been a married man. And Jillian was gone. Once he'd asked Marty where Jillian had moved. Marty had been furious and told him in no uncertain terms that it was none of his business and warned him to leave Jillian alone. She'd moved on with her life. If Miles knew what was good for him, he would do the same. Without Jillian.

Miles had been shocked by the venom in Marty's voice, although in retrospect he shouldn't have been. Marty had been protecting Jillian. Besides, Marty had been right. Miles had forfeited his right to know about Jillian's life. It had taken supreme effort and every ounce of self-discipline he possessed, but he'd left her alone. He'd hoped her marriage had turned out better than his. Now he knew that it hadn't.

"Is that all you're going to say?" he asked her.

"I'm not sure what else there is to say. I never thought of them as belonging to me. No, that's not entirely true. At the time, I thought I had an ownership stake in where you built your house. But that's because I was under the impression that we were going to get married and live in the house together. But once you made it clear that we were not going to be married, I dropped my claim in my heart. You were free to build wherever you wanted to with whoever you wanted to. Including the spots that I preferred."

"That's the thing. I didn't want to live in any of those places with anyone other than you."

Her eyes widened and she gasped. He shouldn't be saying all of this, but he seemed to have lost control of his mouth. Had he been dosed with truth serum? That was the only thing that would explain his sudden need to bare his soul. Rising, he paced to the window and stared out at the view.

"I don't know what to say to that."

He turned back around and walked over to her. "I understand. And to be honest, I'd be happy to end this conversation. I just wanted to let you know what I was thinking at the time."

She nodded and nibbled on her bottom lip. Damn. He'd made her uncomfortable.

Benji and Lilliana walked over to them. Their timing couldn't be better, and he was grateful for the interruption.

"Can we have our snacks now?" Benji asked, leaning against Miles's knee. "We're hungry."

"Snack," Lilliana repeated, giving Miles a sweet smile. She looked so much like Jillian there was no way he could resist her.

"Then let's go eat." They went to the kitchen, stopping in the bathroom to wash their hands, and then he and Jillian lifted the kids onto stools at the center island.

"What are we having?" Jillian asked.

"I think we need a little bit more than snacks," Miles said. "How about grilled cheese and tomato soup?"

"Sounds good," Jillian said. "Do you need help?"

"Nope. But I wouldn't mind."

"Smart aleck." Jillian nudged Miles playfully as she grabbed the cheese and butter from the refrigerator. A slight tingle danced down his spine at the contact and he forced himself to ignore it. They were *friends*. Period.

They'd always kidded around as they worked, making chores so much more fun than when he did them alone, and this time was no different.

He opened two cans of soup while Jillian buttered the bread and placed the slices into a pan. He kept one eye on Jillian and the other on the kids as they played together, rolling the Matchbox cars across the quartz countertop and making a vroom-vroom sound.

Seeing them together made Miles wish that he and Rachel had had more children. Miles and his brothers had always been close, and they'd had a great time growing up. Although Miles wasn't the most outgoing person, when he'd been with his brothers he hadn't needed to be. They'd talked for him. His brothers had kept him from being lonely. With them around, he'd always had someone to play with. He'd tried to replicate that for Benji by taking him to playgroup and enrolling him in skating lessons. For the most part Benji appeared content, but he hadn't made a best friend until Lilliana had come along. She brought him out of his shell.

"How many sandwiches do you want?" Jillian asked.

"I'll take two."

"So will I." She flipped over the sandwiches. As expected, they were a perfect golden brown. The aroma of the cooking bread made his mouth water.

He poured soup into bowls, letting it cool before serving it. While he did that, Jillian put the sandwiches on saucers, cutting the kids' grilled cheese into four triangles each. Miles added green grapes and then poured milk for the kids and grabbed sodas for himself and Jillian.

"This is a great kitchen, Miles," Jillian said, taking a seat at the island. "It's like something out of a magazine."

"Thanks. But I can't take any of the credit. I had

professional help. There's a new designer in Aspen Creek. Her name is April Jones. She moved here from New York a couple of years ago and opened her business. She helped select the floors, lighting and bath and kitchen designs."

"I like her choices. They're beautiful and time-less." She looked through the kitchen to the all but empty adjoining family room. "But what happened in there? Doesn't she do furniture and rugs?"

Miles nodded. "She does. But I don't want my house to look like a showroom."

"You don't have to worry about that."

He laughed. "Cleaning is a breeze, so that's a plus."

"And you can hear your voice echoing, saving you a trip to the mountains. So that's another plus."

"I forgot how funny you are."

"I'm here all week," she joked, flashing a smile.

"Seriously, I don't want my house filled with things that, while beautiful, have no meaning to me. Whatever I put in here will mean something to me and Benji."

"As someone with very little furniture of my own now, I'm not judging." She hesitated. "I sold or donated a good deal of my belongings when I decided to move back home. Not that I had all that much to begin with. What I had wasn't expensive and didn't hold any sentimental value. It was easier to get rid of it than lug it home."

"That makes sense." He swallowed some soup and then continued. "In the meantime, I'm going with the less-is-more style of decorating."

"In this case less is just less."

"Can I have some more milk?" Benji asked.

"Of course," Miles said.

"I want Jilly to get it."

"Sure," she said, taking the cup.

Miles turned his attention back to Jillian. She was always kind and patient with Benji, treating him as lovingly as she treated her daughter. Watching Jillian return Benji's cup gave Miles mixed emotions. He was pleased that Benji felt comfortable turning to Jillian for help, but he didn't want Benji to get too attached. Miles and Jillian were still working on their friendship. Even if they did regain the closeness they'd once shared, Jillian had made it crystal clear that her love for him had died. And it wasn't coming back.

He heard giggling and realized he'd been so busy daydreaming that he'd lost track of time. He glanced up to discover that the kids had finished eating. Jillian had wiped their faces and hands and they were on their way to the family room.

"Well, look who's back with us."

"Sorry."

"Don't be. I understand the need to sneak a little vacation every now and then, even if the only trip you get is when you let your mind wander."

He laughed. "The result of being a single parent."

She nodded and their eyes met. Something indecipherable flashed in hers. Then she blinked and the emotion was gone. The desire to know what feeling she'd just squashed nearly overwhelmed him. He wanted to ask, but he knew he didn't have the right. He'd forfeited that privilege years ago. Sorrow nearly overwhelmed him, and he pushed it aside. Rather than wallow, he stiffened his spine in determination.

He didn't have to accept being consigned to the fringes of Jillian's life. He knew what it was like to be friends with her, and he wanted it back. So he was going to be bold and fight to regain that relationship. But he needed to be smart about it so he didn't lose her forever.

He joined Jillian and the kids for a game of baseball in the family room. Or as close to baseball as it could get when not everyone understood the rules.

Benji was the first batter and he easily hit the ball off the tee. Lilliana clapped and Benji grinned at her.

"Run, Benji," Miles said.

Benji immediately headed for third base. Lilliana giggled and then chased behind him. Suddenly the game of baseball morphed into a cross between tag and a race. Jillian managed to corral Lilliana while simultaneously steering Benji to first base.

Miles put the ball on the tee. "Your turn, Lilliana."

He offered her the bat, but she shook her head. "Ball."

She snatched the ball from the tee and threw it in Benji's direction.

Benji laughed and they chased after the ball. Lilliana grabbed it.

"Let me have the ball, please, so you can take your turn at bat," Miles said.

"No. Ball," Lilliana said.

"Yes, that's a ball. And now it's your turn to hit it. Then you can run."

"No ball."

Miles looked at Jillian. She frowned briefly and then she smiled. "She's saying *snow* ball."

"No ball," Lilliana said, a sweet smile on her face.

"She made a snowman with my father the other day."

"I want to make a snowman," Benji said.

"You up for that?" Miles asked Jillian.

"Sure."

They put on their outerwear and headed out the front door. The lawn was massive and with several inches of fresh snow covering the ground, they would be able to make a huge snowman.

Miles helped Benji and Lilliana make small snowballs and roll them across the ground. Although Lilliana allowed Miles to start the ball, she soon shoved his hands away so she could push the growing ball herself.

Miles shook his head and sat back as she determinedly worked. After a few minutes, her ball was too heavy for her to roll, so she abandoned it and went to help Benji with his. Miles was trying to figure out what to do next when he felt something cold and wet on his neck. He jerked around and came face-to-face with a grinning Jillian. She threw another snowball at him, but he dodged it.

"You know this means war," he said, coming to his feet.

"Naturally."

She pulled her hand from behind her back and sent a snowball whizzing in his direction. In one smooth move, he ducked out of the way, dropped down and quickly packed snow into a ball. He glanced up to see Jillian running for a tree a short distance away. Laughing, he chased her. He threw his snowball in her direction. She laughed as she dodged it and disappeared behind the tree. A few seconds later, a barrage of snowballs came flying his way. While he'd been helping the kids start their snowman, she'd been building her arsenal. She hadn't been retreating. She'd been drawing him into the open so she could attack.

There was only one thing to do.

He scooped some snow and then charged her.

She pelted him with snowballs, but he kept coming. When he was a short distance away, he threw his snowballs at her. They were laughing while they made and threw snowballs as fast as they could, getting closer and closer. When they were mere inches apart, he grabbed her around the waist, keeping her in place when she tried to escape.

"Oh, no, you don't." He held a glove full of snow up to her face.

Her eyes widened. "You wouldn't dare."

"Think not?"

Their chests rose and fell as they took deep, gulping breaths. They were so close that their breath mingled. His eyes were riveted to her face. Puffs of air escaped her slightly parted lips. There was a slight pink tinge to her cheeks and nose. She'd never been more beautiful.

The urge to kiss her was strong and suddenly he couldn't think of a good reason not to.

"So does this mean you give up?" Jillian asked when he didn't move. He shook his head, ridding himself of the dangerous notion he'd had. Kissing Jillian was out of the question.

He turned his hand over and let the snow fall to the ground. He could never smash snow into her face.

She laughed. "I guess that means I win."

"Not so fast there, slick. Why put snow in your face when I can give you a full body freeze?"

"You wouldn't," she repeated, giggling.

"Yes, I would." He leaned in closer. So close that he inhaled her sweet scent. Then he scooped her into his arms and spun in circles. Kneeling, he placed her onto her back in the snow, pinning her hands over her head. "I win. I win."

She laughed and the sound reached inside him, touching his near dead heart. The need to kiss her was too much to resist this time. He lowered his head. His lips were mere inches from touching hers when he felt a weight on his back. Turning, he met two pairs of brown eyes. Then snow hit him in the face.

"We win," Benji exclaimed.

"Win," Lilliana echoed.

Miles and Jillian wiped the snow from their faces, the intimate moment now gone. It was probably for the best. Even so, if the opportunity to kiss Jillian presented itself again, he would act on it in a heartbeat.

Jillian looked at the kids. "Sit down beside me and I'll teach you how to make snow angels."

"Okay," Benji said, coming to sit by Jillian and pushing Miles out of the way in the process.

Jillian lay on her back and then moved her arms and legs over the snow. "Now you try."

The kids immediately mimicked Jillian's actions. Miles watched them for a moment and then joined them. They might be making snow angels, but the way he wanted to kiss Jillian made him more of a snow devil. But it was the best way he knew to cool off.

And he desperately needed to do that right now.

Chapter Ten

Jillian walked Aspen Creek's Main Street, trying to ignore the pink and red hearts that had sprung up overnight in all the shop windows. Valentine's Day was nearly two weeks away and every business in town had caught the romance bug. The restaurants were advertising couples' dinner packages with special menus and urging people to make their reservations now. The florist had enormous bouquets in the window, along with a reminder that time was running out to order flowers for that certain someone. If that wasn't bad enough, the candy shop had gotten into the spirit, showcasing specially designed chocolate assortments. Even the boutiques were warning people that they didn't want to miss out, so buy that perfect outfit today. Jillian wouldn't be surprised if the hardware store and gas station got into the act soon.

She told herself not to be a grump. Nobody liked a Complaining Connie. Besides, she'd once been one of those people who celebrated the day with enthusiasm. Of course, it had been so long since she'd received candy or flowers that she could barely recall how it felt. The first year of her marriage, Evan had treated her to a romantic dinner and bought her a box of chocolates. The next year—nothing. Their marriage had been on the decline by then. This year she was single with no expectation of receiving a gift other than the flowers and card her parents always gave her.

And now she suddenly wanted a gift from Miles, which was ridiculous. They were just friends. But the way they'd interacted at his house the other day had felt like so much more than friendship. She'd wanted to kiss him several times and believed he'd felt the same urge. Thank goodness neither of them had acted on it. They didn't need to repeat mistakes of the past.

But that didn't stop her from wanting something for Valentine's Day. And though she would love to avoid the holiday all-together, that wouldn't be possible. Valentine's Day was the main topic of the Chamber of Commerce meeting.

Reaching the Chamber building, she stepped into the conference room and unbuttoned her coat. About fifteen people of varying ages were gathered around a long table, filling saucers with donuts and mugs with coffee and hot chocolate.

"It's made up anyway, she muttered to herself.

"What's made up?"

She jumped and turned. Miles was standing behind her, an amused grin on his face. He was dressed in dark jeans, a thick sweater and a shearling coat. As usual, he was wearing a black cowboy hat.

"Nothing."

"I can't believe I let Nathan trick me into coming to this meeting."

"That's not the way I remember the conversation going," she pointed out.

"Maybe not, but Nathan is the smartest man I know. He's always two steps ahead of everyone else so you can never be sure."

"We're here now, so we may as well make the best of it. And is it really as bad as all that?"

"It's worse. Are you going to represent the resort from now on?"

"If it's as bad as you say, I hope not. But then, I did kind of volunteer to take over for my mom. And I'm trying to find out where I fit in the company, so who knows?"

"We may as well get something to eat."

"Just coffee for me. I'm meeting my friends for lunch."

They grabbed their refreshments and then found

seats just as the meeting was called to order by George Johnson, owner of the Aspen Creek Candy shop. A former college football player, he was big and burly and as soft-spoken as a man could be.

The minutes of the previous meeting were read and approved. Then they got down to the business at hand: Aspen Creek's Valentine's Day celebration.

They talked about the party for the children, and then they talked about the big fundraiser for charity.

"We would like everyone to contribute something to the raffles," Mr. Johnson said. "The more items we have, the more money we'll raise for the Aspen Creek Angels. And we all know what good work they do."

The Aspen Creek Angels was an organization that provided underprivileged children throughout the state with tickets to sporting events, and activities like skiing and skating lessons their families couldn't afford. They also provided computers and books for kids who needed them.

Jillian raised her hand. When she was recognized, she spoke. "My family's resort will donate a romantic weekend to the raffle."

"What's included?" Dorinda Evans, the secretary asked.

"It's all inclusive. Lift tickets and ski rentals. Spa package. Whatever the winner would like to do. If we offer it, it's available."

"That's very generous," Mrs. Evans said.

Miles offered horseback rides.

"How many?" Mrs. Evans asked.

"Ten lessons. Half an hour in duration each."

After that, other businesses began offering goods and services. There would be many worthy prizes and Jillian knew that they would raise plenty of money for the cause.

Once all the business was wrapped up, the meeting ended.

"That wasn't too bad," Miles said.

"It wasn't. But I don't want to do this every month."

"Neither do I. But I have to admit it was worth it to see Nathan so flustered."

They put on their coats and then left.

"Where are you meeting your friends?"

"At the café."

"I'll walk a couple of blocks with you. I need to stop at the feed store while I'm in town."

As they walked down the street, Jillian glanced out of the corner of her eyes at Miles and her heart stalled. Even after all this time and everything they'd been through, there was something about him that appealed to her. Her brain knew that it was dangerous to allow herself to be attracted to someone who didn't want her, but her heart hadn't gotten the message.

"So, are you going to buy a raffle ticket?" She asked.

"For what?"

"For a chance of winning the big prize. If you want to create special memories with your Valentine, you should get your ticket before they're all gone. Of course, you can always buy a package at the resort."

"My Valentine?"

"Yes. You know, that special someone in your life. The woman who makes your heart go pitter-patter." She managed to keep her voice steady even though the very thought of Miles being involved with another woman made her queasy. She might be capable of being friends with him, and comfortable laughing and joking with him, but her heart still ached when she realized that friends were all they could ever be. She needed to learn to deal with the disappointment.

"I'll keep that in mind." His voice sounded odd, but she couldn't put a finger on the emotion there.

They reached the corner. The diner was straight ahead, but Miles needed to go in the other direction to reach the feedstore.

"I'd better hurry. My friends will be waiting for me. I'll see you later."

"Enjoy your lunch," Miles said and then crossed the street.

Jillian forced herself not to stare as he walked away. She shook herself and picked up her pace. Courtney only had an hour before she had to get back to work.

Jillian's friends were stepping inside the restaurant just as she arrived. They hugged each other and then grabbed a booth near the window. It was past one o'clock so they'd missed the rush. A waitress brought their menus and then promised to be back in a few minutes to take their orders.

"Was that Miles I saw you talking to?" Erica asked.

"What do you mean? You saw us?"

"Yes. I was across the street. And if you were trying to be inconspicuous, you might want to avoid having a rendezvous on Main Street in the middle of the day."

"I'll keep that in mind. But to answer your question, yes, that was Miles. We both went to the Chamber of Commerce meeting. We walked together because we were going in the same direction. And we're friends."

Erica and Courtney exchanged glances.

"You know that I saw that, right?" Jillian said.

Erica laughed. "I'm trying to wrap my mind around the idea that you and Miles are friends again."

"Our kids like each other."

Erica held up her hands in front of her chest. "No need to get defensive. I think it's great that the two of you have put the past behind you. This may be a bit selfish, but it makes my life easier."

"Mine, too," Courtney added.

"What do you mean?"

"Miles and I always got along. He was part of our group. Once the two of you broke up, the circle was broken. We probably wouldn't have known Miles even existed if not for you. When you left it seemed disloyal to invite him to our parties or hang out with him."

Jillian nodded and for a moment she felt a twinge of guilt. Miles was quiet by nature, and it was easy for him to be overlooked. Making friends had been difficult for him but it was as natural as breathing for Jillian. After they'd broken up, it had seemed right that he would no longer be a part of her friend group. To be honest, she had hoped he would continue to be an outcast even after she'd moved to Kansas. Only now did she realize how unfair she'd been.

"Well, we're friends now so he can be a part of the group again. That is, if he wants to be."

"If he wants to be? Who wouldn't want to hang out with us?" Erica asked, a saucy smile on her face.

"Good point," Jillian said.

"Now that you and Miles have buried the hatchet, it's time to get you back into the dating game," Courtney said. "And I know just the man."

Jillian held up her hands, trying to stop her friend before she got on a roll. "Thanks, but no. The last thing I need in my life is a new man."

"Then how do you plan to get over the old one?"

"I am so over Evan that it's not funny. There's something about being told that marriage with me wasn't fun that killed whatever love I might have had for the man."

"I wasn't talking about Evan. We were never convinced that he was anything more than your rebound guy. Or rather, your way to show Miles that you were over him."

Jillian frowned. Her mother had said the very same thing. "How did everyone but me know that?"

"You were too heartbroken to think straight."

"You know, I had been blaming Evan for the way our marriage ended, when the truth was, we were both at fault. We should never have gotten married. I need to stop blaming people for my mistakes."

"Agreed." Courtney lifted her water glass and they toasted.

They went on to discuss other matters. Jillian thoroughly enjoyed herself while they laughed and ate. It was always fun hanging with her girls. They were open and honest with each other without being brutal. Jillian had a new view of the past and realized that she owed many people apologies. Miles, of course, was top of the list. But her girlfriends were deserving also.

Erica and Courtney were getting up from the table when Jillian stopped them. "Before we go, I need to say something."

Erica and Courtney looked at each other again.

"I owe you both an apology."

"For what?" Erica asked.

"For the way I acted. I shouldn't have made you choose between me and Miles. You should have been able to maintain your friendships with both of us. I was wrong to tell you that if you even mentioned him, I would cut you out of my life. That was really immature. I was being a poor friend."

"Agreed," Courtney said.

"You didn't have to agree so readily," Jillian said with a laugh.

"You might have been wrong, but we understood. And it's so good to have you back home. The past is over. Maybe you and Miles have a second chance," Erica said.

She shook her head. "No. We're doing good just to be friends. There's no going back."

"Don't say no so fast. I mean, you're single and so is he. Maybe the timing was just wrong before."

"Timing wasn't the problem. It was the fact that he didn't want to marry me." She sucked in a painful breath and then continued. "Besides, the timing isn't any better now. I'm a single mother trying to get back on my feet. I don't even have a home of my own."

"Are you looking to move out?" Courtney asked. As one of the top real estate agents in the state, she would know of any available properties.

Jillian shrugged. "Not immediately. Lilliana is just getting settled at my parents' house. And to be honest, it's nice having the help."

"Built-in babysitters. Don't think for a minute that I'm letting you off the hook," Courtney said. "I think you and my friend Blake will make the perfect couple. He's new to town and looking to meet new people."

"Then why don't you date him?" Jillian asked.

"He's not my type. And you could use someone to help you move on from Miles."

"I tried that once. It didn't end so well, remember?"

"But you aren't running from a broken heart this time. You're open to meeting new people, aren't you? You don't want to spend the rest of your life alone."

"I would like to think that I've learned from my past mistakes."

"Nobody is saying you have to marry him. Meet him. See if you like him."

"Let me think about it."

"Don't think about it too long. If you're serious about moving forward, then you're going to have to act."

Jillian nodded. That was true. But was she really putting the past behind her, or was she running away from the present? And Miles. Until she knew the answer to those questions, it was best not to act.

Miles shut the door to his sleeping son's room and then returned to the living room. He dropped onto the couch and closed his eyes. This had been a hectic day with so much to do and too little time to do it. Benji had been a little bit clingy today, and once more Miles wished he had a partner in parenthood. Immediately images of Jillian popped in his mind as he recalled the day she'd been there. Although he and Benji were a family, a crew of two as Miles liked to say, Jillian and Lilliana's presence had shown just what they were missing. Perhaps the crew could be increased to four.

But that would mean taking a risk. A risk that could mean losing Jillian's friendship forever this time. He knew what he stood to lose if she rejected his overture and walked away. The past couple of years had driven that fact home. Then he considered all he had to gain. If things worked out, he would regain more than Jillian's friendship. He would win back her love and her heart. And since he'd somehow fallen in love with her again, that was definitely a risk worth taking. If he succeeded, he would be gentle with her heart. He'd be so much more careful to love her the way she deserved.

He picked up the phone. She'd been friendly this afternoon, so perhaps she would be open to talking with him tonight. He scrolled through the contacts until he got to Jillian's info. There was a slight pang in his chest as it struck him once more that she'd changed her number. It was proof that she'd put him firmly out of her life once and a warning that she could do it again. Of course, she'd been married so he understood. He'd been married, too, and it would have been wrong for him to reach out to her. And he hadn't. He'd put all of his effort into his marriage even after he'd realized that by marrying Rachel he'd committed the mistake he'd been trying to avoid. Although he hadn't admitted it to anyone, he'd been relieved when she had told him she was leaving. If she hadn't, he would have suffered through a miserable marriage. He'd made his bed and he'd been resigned to lie in it.

He heard the phone ringing and he put his past out of his mind and waited for Jillian to answer.

"Did I catch you at a bad time?" he asked after she said hello. Her voice sounded slightly breathless, as if she'd been running.

"No. I just made a mug of hot chocolate and I'm settling in front of a roaring fire to enjoy it."

The image she painted was so vivid he could practically see her.

"Ah. I'm jealous."

"Why? You have a fireplace. And a stove. And I know you know how to make hot chocolate."

He closed his eyes. He remembered all of the times they'd spent skiing or enjoying other outdoor sports at her family's resort. They would stay outside until their teeth were chattering and they were practically frozen. Then they'd race inside and make a huge pot of hot chocolate and sit in front of the fire in her family room. Life had been good. "I do. But somehow, mine never tastes as good as yours."

"That's because you always boil the milk. That's a no-no."

He laughed and leaned back against the couch and put his feet up on the coffee table. It had been way too long since he and Jillian had spent time just shooting the breeze. His heart slowed into a relaxed beat. "Perhaps you need to teach me again."

"I don't know. I tried before and it didn't work."

"I'll be a much better student this time around."

"Is that right?"

"Yes."

"You expect me to just take your word for it? I'm not sure I can do that."

"I've changed. Let me prove it to you." Although on the surface they were talking about hot chocolate, he knew they were talking about something much deeper, too.

"How do you intend to do that?"

"I guess I'll just have to show you. The sooner the better. How about we make some hot chocolate tomorrow. Followed by dinner."

"Hmm. I'm not too sure."

He heard the worry in her voice and knew he needed to press his advantage. "If you won't do it for me, do it for Benji."

"What does Benji have to do with anything?"

"Surely you wouldn't want Benji to go another

day without enjoying your super tasty hot chocolate."

"So you're going to use your sweet son and my affection for him to get your way."

"I'm a desperate man, Jillian. I'll do whatever it takes to win."

There was a long silence. Not for the first time he wished he possessed the gift of gab. Since he didn't, he was forced to wait until she replied.

"I suppose that would be all right. What time?"

"How about five thirty. And it goes without saying that you should bring Lilliana."

"It's a date."

He hung up the phone and smiled. He had a date with Jillian.

Chapter Eleven

"What do you mean you and Lilliana have plans?" Jillian asked her mother the next afternoon. This was the first that she was hearing of it. At breakfast, Jillian had mentioned that she and Lilliana were going to have dinner with Benji and Miles. Valerie had simply smiled and told them to have fun. Now she was springing this on her.

"Just what I said. There's a grandparents and grandkids outing this evening in the park field house. They have these events from time to time. This is my first opportunity to go."

For a reason that made absolutely no sense, Jillian felt a twinge of guilt for having denied her mother the opportunity to enjoy these events in the past. Valerie was clearly excited and Jillian didn't have the heart to ruin her mother's plans with her only grandchild.

"We're having hot dogs, pizza and chips and then watching a movie," Valerie continued enthusiastically. "Everyone's going to be there."

Jillian couldn't help but smile at that last part. "But Benji will be expecting to see her tonight."

"And he will. Michelle is bringing him. We've already got plans to sit together."

"Oh. I guess I'll call Miles and cancel."

"Why?"

Jillian blinked, flustered. "It was supposed to be the four of us."

"So now it will be the two of you. I don't see the problem."

Naturally she wouldn't. Valerie had always liked Miles and been enthralled by the idea of her daughter marrying her best friend's son. Jillian wondered if her mother still harbored that dream. She certainly hoped not. Love and marriage weren't in the cards for Jillian and Miles.

"I'm not sure Miles will want me to come alone. Now that he has a free night, he might make other plans."

"Well, call and ask him."

Jillian pulled out her phone, wondering how something so logical could sound like a challenge. As the phone rang, her heart sped up and she couldn't decide if she wanted Miles to reschedule or not. Would she be relieved or disappointed if he told her not to come?

Before she could decide, he answered. "Hey. I was just thinking about you."

She told her foolish heart not to read too much into his words. It skipped a beat in defiance of her order. "I hope they were good thoughts."

"I don't know anything about you that's not good."

She smiled and it took a moment for her to get back on track. "I'm calling because my mother just informed me that she and your mother are taking the kids to some event at the park tonight."

"Yeah. I forgot all about it. Benji always has a blast at those things. I'm sure Lilliana will have a great time, too."

"So what about tonight? Do you want to reschedule?"

"No way. I dreamed about that hot chocolate all night. Why? Do you want to?"

"No. I'm game if you are."

"Then come over as planned. I'll switch up the menu from chicken fingers and tater tots to something a bit more grown-up."

"What are you going to make?"

"That's for me to know and you to find out."

Jillian laughed. Miles knew that she didn't like secrets. It would gnaw at her until she walked into the door and smelled the aromas floating on the air. "Fine. Be that way. I'll see you later."

"Later."

Anticipation grew as Jillian went about her day. Although she told herself that she was simply having dinner with an old friend, she couldn't force herself to put on the well-worn jeans and casual top she'd planned to wear when the children were going to be around. Instead, she dressed in black slacks, black boots and a cream sweater with silver threads that hugged her curves. Calling herself all kinds of fool, she put on makeup, jewelry and misted on her favorite perfume.

Her parents and Lilliana had already left, so she didn't have to explain to anyone why she had gone to such lengths with her appearance. Heck, she was still trying to come up with an explanation that she believed herself. As she drove to Miles's ranch, she decided she didn't need one.

She parked, darted up the stairs and rang the bell.

"Come inside where it's warm," Miles said, as he opened the door.

"You don't have to tell me twice," Jillian said, unwinding the red scarf from around her neck. She removed her coat and placed it in Miles's outstretched hand, then fluffed her hair over her shoulders.

"I'm in the kitchen setting the table. You can keep me company." He held out a hand, signaling for Jillian to go ahead of him. His hand brushed against the small of her back, sending shivers tripping down her spine. *Calm down, Jillian. You don't want to make a fool of yourself.*

She stepped into the kitchen and looked around. There were two place settings at the table. A floral arrangement and candles made a beautiful centerpiece. A fire was blazing in the fireplace in the family room, and she approached its welcoming warmth.

Holding out her hands, she stole a glance over her shoulder at Miles. He looked scrumptious in navy slacks and a gray sweater that emphasized his muscular physique. She was glad she'd paid extra attention to her appearance.

Miles joined her by the fire. He was freshly shaved, and when he came nearer, she got a whiff of his aftershave. He smelled so good that she wanted to lean in closer, but that was out of the question. She'd be disappointed if Miles led her on. She'd be pissed if she misled herself.

"I really need to get some furniture in here. At least a couch or a chair to sit on."

"Did your ex-wife take a lot of things when she left?"

He shook his head. "Rachel never lived in this house."

"She didn't?" Jillian didn't know why that filled

her with relief, but it did. Even so, it didn't change things between her and Miles.

"No. Nathan has a small house on the far side of the ranch. He spends so much time on the road that I don't think he's slept there more than a handful of times. We lived there when we first got married. I wanted a house of our own. I thought that might make things better between us. She wasn't interested in the process, so I did everything on my own. By the time the house was finished, so were we."

"Oh."

"Yeah. Oh." He was silent for a moment and then he looked at Jillian, an unreadable expression in his eyes. "But I don't want to talk about Rachel. She's part of my past. And the past doesn't interest me."

"What do you want to talk about?"

"The present. The future. Anything but the past. It can't be changed so there's no sense wasting time talking about it."

"But we can learn from it."

"Do people really learn from the past?"

"I hope so." She also hoped she would be wiser in the future when it came to affairs of the heart. Especially where Miles was concerned. She didn't want to make the mistake of falling in love with him a second time, but she didn't seem to have control over that. The best she could hope for was that her heart wouldn't be that foolish yet again.

* * *

Miles could have spent the rest of the night staring at Jillian, but there was dinner to get on the table. When his mother had reminded him that she and his father had plans with Benji tonight, and that Lilliana would be spending the evening with her grandparents, he'd decided to make the most of the opportunity by serving a romantic dinner for two. Too bad he didn't possess the skills to prepare the kind of meal Jillian deserved.

He knew that she loved all kinds of seafood. Lucky for him, Aspen Creek had several top-tier restaurants. Even luckier, a friend from high school was the head chef at one. Lionel had prepared a special meal and then he'd given Miles detailed instructions on cooking everything. He'd also recommended a bottle of wine to compliment the meal.

"You know, I don't smell anything cooking," Jillian said, a perplexed expression on her face. "You did invite me for dinner, correct?"

"Yes. And hot chocolate."

"I agreed to make the hot chocolate, but I didn't agree to cook."

"Not to worry. I've got it handled."

"Did you order pizza?"

"Nope."

He stood and held out a hand. She took it. Her skin was soft and warm, and he felt a shock of electricity at the contact. Her soft gasp let him know she'd felt it, too. The urge to kiss her was great, but he squashed the impulse. Jillian wasn't ready for where that might lead. To be honest, neither was he. They'd always gone up in flames with the slightest contact, but they needed to be wiser now.

Ignoring the voice telling him to take things to the next level, he dropped her hand. "After you."

She nodded and he could have sworn that he saw disappointment in her eyes. But then she smiled and he decided that he'd imagined her reaction.

She took a seat at the island and then looked around. "I'm not seeing a single pot. Please don't tell me we're having peanut butter and jelly sandwiches."

He laughed. "No. I learned my lesson."

"I'm glad to hear it. No girl wants to be invited to dinner and be served peanut butter and jelly sandwiches."

"To be fair, I was twelve."

"That's true. And the chips and cookies were good, so that's a plus."

"I guess I should have asked if you liked jelly before I'd made the sandwiches. But who doesn't like jelly?"

"Not all jelly. Just grape. And just so you know, I'm not a fan of crunchy peanut butter, either."

"Luckily we're not having that."

"What are we having?"

He opened the refrigerator and began pulling out several foil containers with cardboard tops. "For starters, we're having bacon-wrapped scallops with spicy cilantro mayonnaise followed by lobster bisque. For our main course we'll enjoy lobster tails, baked potatoes and steamed broccoli."

"That sounds delicious. And just how do you plan to pull it off?"

"Do you remember Lionel Griffin from high school?"

She nodded.

"He's head chef at Under the Seafood Restaurant in town. He did the prep work and gave me directions on how to prepare it. Dinner will be served soon."

"I'm impressed." Jillian looked so pleased that he was glad he'd gone all out for this dinner. He opened the bottle of wine and poured them each a glass.

"How about some music?" she asked, holding up her phone.

"Good idea. I'll hook it up to the speakers via Bluetooth." He took the phone and pressed a couple of buttons. Before long, the music from one of her playlists was playing through unseen speakers in the kitchen.

"Nice. I'm going to have to add wireless speakers to the list of things I want in my dream house."

"Are you building new?"

"Right now, I'm not doing anything. But when

the time comes, I want to have everything figured out in terms of decor. I'm starting my list now, so I don't forget anything essential."

"Since when did you become a planner? What happened to the spontaneous woman you used to be?"

"She's still in there. Somewhere. Every now and then she pops out just to keep things interesting. But when it comes to a major investment like a house, I'm less spontaneous."

"I remember the lists you used to make when I was talking about building a house." He probably shouldn't have mentioned that time because of how their relationship ended, but they couldn't avoid tough discussions. Their past was complicated. They'd been major parts of each other's lives for years—both for good and bad. As much as he wished otherwise, those hard times couldn't be erased. They couldn't pretend the past away, so they were going to have to deal with it straight on.

She twisted her fingers, and he regretted his words. Timing was everything, and his appeared to be off. No surprise there. He'd never been smooth. He was trying to come up with something—anything—to say when she spoke.

"I guess I should apologize for that."

Of all the things she could have said, he hadn't expected that. "Apologize? Why? For what?"

"Because you were looking for a place to build

your house and I hijacked the entire project. You had only mentioned that you were thinking of moving out of your parents' house and I was off and running. As usual."

"You didn't hijack anything. I was happy for your suggestions. Quiet as it's kept, I like your zeal."

She laughed, but it wasn't the merry sound he associated with her. "That's one word for it. Pushy is another one."

He shoved the food into the oven and then came and sat beside her. Taking her hand in his, he gave it a gentle squeeze, and she lifted her head until their eyes met. "You might have been a little pushy, but I needed that push. If not for you, I wouldn't have had nearly as much fun as I did. I certainly wouldn't have made the number of friends that I have and wouldn't have been invited to the parties and gatherings that I attended. Because of you, my life was much fuller and happier than it would have been otherwise. I'm grateful for the push."

"Really?"

He'd never seen her so unsure. The doubt in her voice was heartbreaking. She'd been the best part of his life. Why hadn't he realized that before? If he had known then what he knew now, she wouldn't have gotten away from him. "Really."

"Then I'm glad I was able to get you out of your shell."

"So am I. I know this wasn't one of the places

you suggested, but what do you think of this location?"

"I have to admit it's nice. You have a great view of the mountains."

"You can't tell now because everything is covered with snow, but in the spring and summer the land out back is gorgeous. The grass is so green and in the distance you can see the wildflowers blowing in the breeze. It's really quite scenic."

"I can imagine. And even though you didn't choose my location, you did go with one of the models I liked."

"I'm not an entire fool."

She laughed and this time it was filled with joy. He blew out a relieved breath. They'd faced one awkward moment and come out as friends. That was a positive sign.

They chatted while the food cooked. When it was done, they worked together to plate it. He led her to the table, pleased by the way the flowers and candles looked. She smiled when he held out her chair for her and the blood pulsed in his veins in response.

"Isn't this fancy?"

"Nothing but the best for you."

"Stop talking like that or you'll turn my head."

"Would that be so bad?"

"It would be the worst." She spoke quietly, but he could tell she hadn't been joking. The pain in her voice was mixed with something else. Fear.

"Why?"

"Because, Miles, there is no future for us. We tried before and it was a catastrophe. I don't want to give my heart to someone when I know it will only be rejected."

"What makes you think that will happen?"

"The past is a great predictor of the future."

"I wasn't rejecting your heart before, Jillian." He didn't know how many times he had to say this before she believed him. "I just wanted to be sure that I loved you."

"There's no need to rehash the past. Especially now when it doesn't make a difference. I'm not in the position to fall in love with you or anyone else. I'm not sure I want to be in love again. I'm trying to rebuild my life as a single mother. Lilliana has to be my main focus right now. You know?"

He nodded. He was in the same position. "Did I just ruin things? Trust me, I want this dinner to be fun."

"You didn't ruin anything. It's good that we cleared the air. Now we just need a reset." She lifted her wine glass in toast. "To starting this dinner over on the right foot."

He lifted his glass and clinked it against hers. "I can do that."

They sipped and when they set their glasses down the mood had actually shifted. As they ate, they laughed and teased each other as they'd done when they'd been best friends, proof that things could be good between them.

"That was really delicious," Jillian said after she'd eaten the last morsel. "I can't remember when I've had a better meal."

He dipped his head, accepting her praise. "Thanks. I'll be sure to pass on your words to the chef."

"I don't think I can eat another bite."

"Oh, no, you don't. You're not getting out of making that hot chocolate you promised me."

She smiled. "I have no intention of backing out. I just need to make a bit of space in my stomach."

"Do you want to go for a walk?"

"I wouldn't mind a short one."

They quickly dressed in their coats and boots, then he led her through the back patio door. She looked around and then smiled. "This is spectacular."

"Once I started on the house, I decided to go all out. We're forty-five minutes from town here, so I added all of the amenities that I can't enjoy without making the long trip."

"So you built your own oasis. I like the in-ground pool and hot tub. How much use do you actually get out of them?"

"Not much this time of year. But in the summer? I usually get in some laps before Benji wakes up.

And the hot tub does wonders on my aching back and shoulders after a long day."

They crossed the brick patio. The snow was compacted, making walking easier. She'd always been steady on her feet, but to be on the safe side, he took her hand. Though they were both wearing gloves, he imagined he could feel the warmth from her hand.

"I think I might have to change my mind," she said after about ten minutes.

"About what?"

"This might be a better place to build your house than any of the places that I liked."

"What makes you say that?"

"Even under all of this snow, this view is spectacular. I can only imagine how beautiful it will be in the summer when the trees are green. And in the fall when the leaves turn colors."

"You don't have to imagine. You only have to wait until a little while longer. Then you can come over and see for yourself."

"Are you planning on throwing a big party?"

"I wasn't. I was thinking about the two of us. The four of us if we don't have babysitters for Lilliana and Benji."

"No worries there. My parents are so thrilled to have Lilliana around they don't know how to act. And she's enjoyed being spoiled by them. There's nothing like grandparent love."

"Same here. I feel guilty about saying it, but there are times when I want a break from my son."

"You're not alone. I try to remind myself that there's nothing wrong with wanting time to myself. I'm a better mother when I'm not stressed."

He nodded.

"And Lilliana needs a community of people, not just me."

"That's something I'm still learning," he admitted. "Benji really drew into himself when his mother left. He cried a lot and started sucking his thumb. I did everything I knew to reassure him that I wasn't going to leave. I might have gone a bit overboard."

"You wouldn't be the first parent to do that. And everything you did was out of love."

He nodded, too moved for words.

She stepped in front of him. "I know I told you this before, but her leaving is a reflection of her. Not you."

"I appreciate you saying that."

"But do you believe it?"

"When you say it, I do."

"Then I'll have to keep saying it." She stepped beside him, grabbed his hand and then started walking again.

The sun had long since set, turning the sky into a dark blue blanket filled with hundreds of bright stars that lit their path. Not that he needed light.

He'd grown up on this ranch and knew every inch of it like the back of his hand.

A peace suffused him and he inhaled deeply. He hadn't felt this at ease in the longest time. Not since before his friendship with Jillian had ended. When she'd left, there had been a hole in his heart that nothing and no one else could fill. And he had tried. Now that she was back the hole was gradually healing.

He tugged on her hand. Her cheeks had taken on a red tint, and she was starting to tremble. In another minute her teeth would be chattering. "Come on. You're getting cold. Let's go back inside. I believe there are hot drinks in our future. And I have to confess that I can't wait to taste that hot chocolate."

"I bet."

"Everything that we need is in the kitchen. And I even picked up some cookies from Bake it Up."

"Chocolate chip?" Jillian's eyes lit up at the prospect.

"Would I dare serve you anything else?"

"Not if you expect me to make my special hot chocolate for you."

Once they were back inside, they headed for the fire so they could warm up. The fire was burning low, so Miles added another log, getting the fire roaring again. Jillian blew on her hands and then sat on them, trying to warm her fingers more quickly.

She stretched her stockinged feet toward the fire, in an attempt to knock the chill from her toes.

Not giving it a second thought, he sat across from her and settled her feet on his lap. He removed her thick socks and then began to rub her feet, starting at the toes and working toward her heels. Her feet were cold, yet her skin was soft. Delicate. He glanced at her face. She'd let her head fall back slightly, and her face was lifted to the ceiling. Her eyes were closed in bliss. A sigh escaped her parted lips and he was immediately aroused. It was a mistake to continue touching her, but he couldn't make himself stop.

It had been several long years since he'd been this close to Jillian. Empty years. Of their own volition, his hands traveled from her now warm feet past her ankles and to her calves. They were strong and shapely, and heaven to touch.

"Uh, I'm warm," Jillian said softly, pulling her legs away from his touch and slipping her socks on. "Thanks."

"No worries." His voice was husky, and he cleared his throat and tried again. He needed to ease the sexual tension bubbling between them and keep the moment light. "I can't have you getting frostbite."

"Not if you want your hot chocolate," she said with a smile.

"And you know I do."

He helped Jillian to her feet and let her precede him to the kitchen. He took a couple of deep breaths before following her.

Jillian immediately set about making their beverage. To his way of thinking, her hot chocolate was good enough to serve as dessert and the cookies were just a bonus. Jillian had always had a sweet tooth and he couldn't imagine that time had changed that. Though they'd been apart for years, he was discovering that he had forgotten very little of her likes and dislikes. He'd simply filed them away while he was married. Now, though, every detail he'd learned over the years came rushing back and he intended to use that knowledge to his full advantage.

There was something so peaceful about leaning against the counter, watching as she stirred the pan of milk. When she was satisfied that it had reached the proper temperature, she added chunks of chocolate, poured in vanilla and dropped in a bit of cinnamon. The aroma was enticing, and his mouth began to water in anticipation.

She gave him a look. "Don't you think it's about time for you to warm up the cookies?"

He was having too good a time staring at her to move. She possessed a quiet elegance that contrasted with her outgoing nature. Jillian was nothing if not contradictory.

"The cookies will only take thirty seconds in the microwave."

"The chocolate will be done in a minute, cowboy, so get a move on."

"Yes, ma'am," he said.

While the cookies heated, he grabbed mugs from the cabinet. Jillian poured in the chocolate and then topped it off with whipped cream and full-size marshmallows. He took one of the mugs and the plate of cookies. She pulled a few paper towels from the roll and grabbed her mug. By unspoken agreement, they returned to the fire.

"This is nice," Jillian said, leaning back on her elbows.

"I agree." Nice was an understatement. This was heaven on earth.

She bit into a cookie and closed her eyes in ecstasy. "Delicious."

While Jillian's eyes were closed, Miles took the opportunity to look at her face. She was just so beautiful. With perfectly clear skin, high cheekbones and full lips, she had the face of a beauty queen. Her hat had smashed her hair, but even though it was no longer perfectly coiffed, it was gorgeous to him and he longed to run his hands through her thick black curls.

She took another bite of her cookie and chewed it. There was something erotic about the way her lips moved, and Miles couldn't look away to save his life. A smear of chocolate dotted the corner of her mouth and he longed to reach out and wipe it away. But he wouldn't. Couldn't. That was too intimate. He picked up his hot chocolate, took a drink and then groaned in pleasure.

She opened her eyes. They sparkled with amusement as she looked at him. "I take it I haven't lost my touch."

"No. You still have it." He pointed to the chocolate on her mouth. "And you still can't eat cookies without sharing them with your whole face."

The pink tip of her tongue darted out as she attempted to remove the stain. "Did I get it all?"

"For the most part."

"What does that mean? You better not let me leave here with food all over my face. So if there's more, let me know."

"I can do better than that," he said. Despite the myriad reasons he shouldn't touch her, he reached out and wiped the remaining chocolate from her lips. Her mouth was soft and tantalizing. She sucked in a breath and then froze. Her eyes flew to his and he held her gaze briefly before he dropped his hand and looked away. They'd already started this evening over once. He didn't think she'd give him another chance if he stepped out of line.

He sipped more of his drink, and she did the same. They stared into the fire, each keeping their thoughts private. In the past he would have relied on her to get the conversation restarted, but he took the reins this time. "I missed this."

"My chocolate? I wrote the recipe down for you years ago. All you have to do is follow it."

"Is that what you call a recipe? I mean, 'add vanilla until it smells right, or cinnamon until it looks right' isn't exactly scientific. And 'let the ancestors guide you' isn't as clear a direction as you think."

She laughed and shook her head. "I see your point. I'll try to recreate it with better measurements for your future use."

"I'd appreciate that. But that's not what I meant."

"What did you mean?"

"I meant I missed this." He waved his hand between them. "Us. I missed being with you. Our friendship. And more."

"More?"

"I miss our relationship. I miss being in love."

She looked at him for a moment before she replied. When she spoke, her voice was soft. Uncertain. "Were we in love? I know that I was in love with you, but you weren't sure you were in love with me. Remember?"

"I do."

"Then what are you saying? It's as if you're trying to rewrite history. I wanted to marry you. I wanted to have children and create a family and a home. But you weren't sure that I was the right one for you. After all the years we'd been together you had doubts.

"When you said that you wanted to have a serious conversation, I thought that meant you wanted to propose to me. Imagine my shock when you told me you wanted to see other women."

At the time, he hadn't known that she'd expected a proposal that night, but he'd started to suspect that she was thinking along those lines. That was why he'd wanted to have that conversation with her. "I just needed time. I didn't want to lead you on when I had so many doubts about our future. You deserved a man who was one hundred percent sure that he could be the man you needed."

"Agreed." She'd finished her drink and cookies, leaving only crumbs on the plate. She inhaled and then looked at him. "Miles, the past is over. I understand why you did what you did. And for the most part I don't harbor any negative feelings."

"For the most part?"

She shrugged. "I'm a work in progress. When my rational mind is in control of my feelings, I know that you did the right thing. The last thing I want is to be married to someone who doesn't love me. I had that with Evan and it was not fun. And strange as this may sound, it would have been worse with you."

"Why is that?"

"Because I loved you more than I ever loved

Evan. He hurt me when he left. But as bad as it was, most of the pain was because I knew that Lilliana was going to miss out by not having her father. But you…you had the ability to decimate me. It hurt having you break up with me when we were only dating. But a broken marriage between us would have destroyed me. I never could have come back from that."

There was nothing he could say to take away her pain. He had to sit with the knowledge that he'd hurt her.

"But like I said, I'm okay now. I'm actually enjoying becoming your friend again. And I'm pleased with where I am in my life now. I don't need to fall in love again to be happy. I meant it when I said I'm not looking for love now. I don't know if I'll ever fall in love again."

"Don't say that."

"Why? Can you honestly tell me you're willing to put your heart on the line again?"

"With the right woman. In a heartbeat." But she'd ruled that out. At least for now. "I just don't want to be the cause of you giving up on love."

"You aren't. At least not in the way that you mean. Relationships don't always work out. Ours didn't. I think friendship is the best way to go. At least between us. Don't you agree?"

He was still trying to think of an appropriate answer when she stretched. His eyes were immediately drawn to her breasts. He was as attracted to her as he'd ever been. He probably always would be.

Things had always been so easy between them. He didn't know why he'd thought that was wrong. That love was supposed to take work. Isn't that what everyone always said—that relationships were hard work? But things had never been hard with Jillian.

"I suppose I need to get going," she said. "We both need to get up early in the morning."

He glanced at the clock. Wow. It was late. Hours had passed but they'd felt like minutes.

She was on her feet, mug in one hand and balled-up paper towels in the other, before he could think of something to say to delay the inevitable. He grabbed his mug and followed her into the kitchen. "I'll wash these."

"There's extra hot chocolate in the pan for you and Benji."

"I'll refrigerate it and microwave it tomorrow."

"Reheat it in the pan. Slowly. It'll taste better."

"If you say so."

"I do."

They walked to the door and he watched as she put on her boots and coat. He was opening the door to let her out when she turned to him and placed a hand on his chest. His heart began to thud. "I really had a wonderful time, Miles. Thanks so much for inviting me."

She raised on her tiptoes and kissed his cheek.

Heat blazed through him and, as she pulled away, he wrapped his arm around her waist, pulling her back to him. Her eyes widened in surprise, but she didn't resist. He took that as a positive sign. Slowly he lowered his head and brushed his lips across hers. Her mouth was soft and warm and held the promise of all that was good in the world.

He'd intended to keep the kiss brief, and although it started as tentative, he soon gave way to the desire that had been building inside him all night. Her lips moved beneath his and he licked the seam of her mouth. She opened to him and he swept his tongue inside. She tasted so sweet. Like chocolate and cinnamon and the sweetness that belonged exclusively to her. He deepened the kiss, pressing her body up against his. Her curves were soft and delectable. Nothing had ever felt this good.

The need to carry her upstairs to his bedroom and make love to her was growing stronger by the moment. He had taken a step in that direction when he became aware that Jillian was pushing against his chest, and he reluctantly released her, ending the kiss.

"That shouldn't have happened," she said.

"Some things are inevitable."

"Even so, we need to learn from the past so we don't repeat our mistakes."

Nodding, he released her. "I hear you." He stepped

aside and opened the door. "Drive carefully. Let me know when you get home."

One thing was certain. This wasn't the end of their relationship. It was the beginning.

Chapter Twelve

What had she done? She'd *kissed* Miles.

She shouldn't have done it. And she definitely shouldn't have enjoyed it as much as she had.

Now that she was alone in her car driving home, she allowed herself to relive the kiss. The sensations were still reverberating through her body. Recalling how wonderful his lips had felt against hers made her shiver again. She inhaled deeply and could practically smell his familiar masculine scent. Memories of the past and how well they'd fit together had taunted her over the last few weeks, rising up when she'd least expected. She'd gone years without thinking of him, convincing herself that she was over him. One scorching kiss had disabused her of that notion. She still wanted him.

Although they'd kept things friendly while they were eating, the walk between them had held an undercurrent of romance. The night had been cold, but being near Miles had helped keep her warm. With the stars shining in the deep blue sky and the moon lighting the path, it was as if she had been thrust into the scene of a movie. She'd always been partial to nighttime, no matter the season, and she'd been enchanted.

Sipping hot chocolate beside him in front of the fire had felt like a dream come true. The soft music playing from the hidden speakers had added to the ambiance. Miles had been so handsome, and she'd sneaked peeks at him whenever he was looking away. For the most part, things had been platonic, and she'd been certain that nothing would happen between them.

She'd been wrong. The two of them had been playing with fire that started when he'd massaged her feet and calves. It had smoldered until they'd kissed. Then it erupted, threatening to become an all-consuming inferno. Thank goodness she'd been able to pull herself back from the brink in time. She might not have the strength in the future. Which was why there couldn't be a next time.

She reached home and pulled her car into the attached garage. Before she stepped into the house, she texted Miles to let him know that she was home. She removed her coat and boots, leaving them in the mud room, then went into the living room. Her mother was sitting beside the fireplace, working on a crossword puzzle. She smiled when she saw Jillian.

"How was your dinner?" Valerie asked.

"It was delicious," Jillian said, choosing to talk about the food instead of the entire evening. "Miles got the food from a new restaurant in town. I think we should give their food a try. We might want to add them to the resort's recommendations list."

"That sounds like a good idea." Valerie gave Jillian a knowing look. Obviously she hadn't been fooled. "I expected you to be home earlier."

"So did I. Lilliana didn't give you a problem, did she?"

"You already know the answer to that ridiculous question. We had a fantastic time. Once she saw Benji she was in hog heaven."

"I bet."

"The two of them reminded me of you and Miles at that age. You two were the best of friends. Completely inseparable."

Before Jillian had fallen so deeply in love with him that no other man could ever compare. "I don't remember all that clearly."

"Of course not. You were in diapers just like Lilliana. But I remember. You two were thick as thieves. I'm so happy that the two of you have put your differences behind you. You need each other."

"It is easier being friends than it is being enemies."

"Of course. But what about something more?"

"You mean like being in love?"

"Not like being in love. Actually being in love."

Jillian thought of the kiss and how wonderful it had felt. How natural. And then she thought of the pain that she'd felt when he'd broken her heart because he hadn't been sure. What if he still wasn't sure?

"That's not something I want to think about."

"Because?"

"I don't know if I trust Miles not to break my heart again."

"How will you know?"

Jillian shrugged. "That's the question. I just wish I knew the answer."

Valerie looked at her as if expecting more. But there was no more to say. Valerie stood and closed her crossword puzzle book, leaving the pencil inside. "And on that note, I think I'll go to bed."

"Good night. I'm going to stay down here for a few more minutes."

Jillian sat by the fire for a while, trying to get a handle on her feelings. She pressed her fingers against her mouth, imagining that she felt Miles's lips moving against hers. She knew she shouldn't, but she wanted one more kiss.

Jillian looked at the red construction paper and did her best to quash her negative feelings. The last thing she wanted to do was work on a Valentine's Day craft. She didn't want to think of romance at all. She glanced at Miles, whose brow was wrinkled, a sign that he'd been caught off guard, too.

"We're going to do something different today," Veronica said. "Valentine's Day is three days away and we thought the kids would get a kick out of making crafts with you. There are two that we're going to do. A card made out of pink, red and white construction paper and a pillow in the shape of a heart."

They took seats at the tables and began to work. Lilliana grabbed a pink heart out of the bin in the center of the table, crushing it.

"Let's be gentle," Jillian said, taking the crumpled paper from her daughter's hand and smoothing it as best she could. After a minute she gave up and grabbed another one.

"Like this?" Benji asked, holding his paper by a corner.

"That's perfect."

Benji beamed and gingerly set the heart on the table. She and Miles helped the children choose and fold construction paper for the cards. As expected,

Lilliana resisted any additional help, holding her paper away from Jillian's hands. "Lily do."

"Okay." Jillian cringed as Lilliana swiped the glue stick over the pink paper, using way more than was necessary and getting a generous amount on the table.

"Good job," Lilliana said to herself. She clapped a few times and then held the paper in the air.

"Good job," Jillian echoed. "Now let's put on the red and white hearts." She took several from the plastic bin and laid them out so Lilliana could choose a few. They were of varying sizes and Lilliana grabbed the biggest one. Although Jillian kept her focus on her daughter and providing what assistance Lilliana would allow, she was acutely aware of Miles sitting across from her. Dressed in faded jeans that emphasized his well-developed thighs and a plaid shirt that hugged his broad shoulders, he was playing havoc with her self-control. She'd lectured herself on the drive to the library this morning, reminding herself to resist his sex appeal. She shouldn't have wasted her time. Miles Montgomery would always be irresistible.

It wasn't just his looks, although his body and face were second to none. It was his personality. His quiet strength. His patience. Even now, as he helped Benji scribble his name on the bottom of the card with an orange marker, he gave Lilliana the attention she demanded, praising her for doing such a wonderful job.

Once the cards were finished, Jillian placed them on a shelf so the glue could dry then joined Miles and the kids at the next station. Making the pillow required more adult assistance than the cards had. Jillian and Miles helped Lilliana and Benji attach the two sides of felt together with yarn. Then they watched as the kids filled the pillow with polyester stuffing. Once the pillows were nearly bursting, she and Miles helped them close the pillows.

Benji and Lilliana were proud of their pillows and pressed them against their chests.

"If that was supposed to be a gift for a special someone, that person is going to be disappointed. You won't be able to pry that pillow from Lilliana's hands if you tried," Miles said.

"Same with Benji," Jillian pointed out.

Once the projects were done, Veronica led the kids to the rug where she read a book about Valentine's Day, while the parents cleaned glue from the tables and chairs and swept bits of paper from the floor. Though they'd been working in different parts of the room, somehow Miles and Jillian ended up next to each other.

"We've got to stop meeting like this," Miles joked.

Jillian smiled. He might be kidding but there was some truth in his words. Being around him wasn't doing her heart any favors. She glanced around at the other parents who were in small clusters around the room. It would be easy for her to join one of those groups to create a safe distance from him, but that was unnecessary. It wasn't as if she and Miles were going to kiss *now*. Or anytime for that matter. They'd agreed that kissing had been a mistake that they weren't going to repeat. But as she recalled how blissful she'd felt in his arms, she couldn't remember why they'd made that decision.

"I know."

"What are you doing to celebrate Valentine's Day?"

"You mean besides this?"

"Yes. Not that anything can top this for excitement."

"I don't have any plans." Other than scarfing down the box of chocolates she'd bought for herself and watching her favorite rom-coms. But she had no intention of sharing that with him.

"Are you going to the Aspen Creek dinner dance?"

She'd thought about it. Her family had bought tickets as usual, and her parents and brothers were going. Marty's company was catering the dinner and he would no doubt hang around for the dance. But Marty being Marty, he'd probably be mobbed by every woman who'd come alone and a couple who hadn't. "I don't think so. Are you?"

He shrugged. "My parents have been pressuring me to get out more. My mother has been dropping hints that this would be the perfect opportunity for me to meet someone." He rolled his eyes.

"Thankfully my mother hasn't gone that far. Yet."

"Do you want to go with me?"

That was abrupt and seemed to come out of nowhere. But then, Miles had never been one to beat around the bush. "I'm not sure I'm even going."

"Come on. It'll be fun."

She just raised her eyebrows. Since when was being around a bunch of happy couples fun? True, she'd been to enough of these dances to know that everyone wasn't paired off. There would be plenty of single men and women mingling and dancing. She just didn't want to be one of them.

Unless… Was he asking her to be his valentine? The thought thrilled her – and made her a bit shaky. If he was, they would be crossing the line separating friendship from romance. A line she wasn't sure she was ready to cross.

"I don't know." She felt herself weakening.

"The food is going to be top-notch."

"If you're hoping to win me over, that argument is not going to work. I can eat Marty's food any day of the week."

"Well, then, consider it a favor for a friend. I'm

afraid my mother will ask someone for me if you don't."

"I know your mother. She's not that bad."

"She *wasn't* that bad. And maybe she wouldn't be if I hadn't become a hermit after my divorce. I stayed by myself way too much. I need to prove to her that I'm not as bad off as I was when Rachel left before she takes out an ad in the newspaper or enters me in that ridiculous bachelor auction."

"What bachelor auction?"

"Somebody in the Chamber of Commerce got the bright idea to hold an auction to raise money for charity. You can buy a date with one of Aspen Creek's most eligible bachelors or some such nonsense. It's supposed to happen one night this summer. I don't know any more details because I don't intend to participate." He waved a hand. "I don't want to talk about that anymore. So back to the question. Will you go with me to the dance?"

"Well…"

"And it would keep your mother off your case."

He had a point. She closed her eyes and took a deep breath. "Fine. I'll go with you."

He gave her a charming smile that curled her toes. "You won't regret it."

Wrong. She already regretted it.

Miles fastened the top button on his white shirt and then put on his tie. For the past two days, he'd debated between sending Jillian a box of expensive chocolates and a bouquet of red roses. Or both. Then he recalled how hard he'd had to work to convince her to be his date and thought the better of it. He didn't want to scare her off by coming on too strong. She'd only agreed to come with him to the dinner dance as his friend. In the end he'd decided to buy her a corsage and to bring her a small box of her favorite chocolate covered strawberries. Surely that wouldn't scare her off. It was Valentine's Day after all.

As he grabbed his jacket, he smiled in anticipation of seeing Jillian again. It felt so good to have her back in his life. This might not be an official date, but he was looking forward to spending time alone with her. There would be dancing, and he would be able to hold her in his arms without raising her alarms. And who knew, if luck was with him, tonight could lead to an official date.

After tying his tie, he headed downstairs where his teenage babysitter sat at the kitchen table with Benji. Crystal was the daughter of one of the ranch hands and he'd known her for most of her life. More importantly, Benji was comfortable with her. Miles had bought pizza for them and soda for Crystal.

"Your mother came over and brought us cookies. She said to ask if Benji can have one or two. Can he?" Crystal asked.

"Sure. That would be okay." He opened the refrigerator and grabbed the clear plastic box containing Jillian's corsage.

He kissed Benji's head. "Be a good boy for Crystal, okay?"

"Okay, Daddy," Benji said, picking a piece of pepperoni from the pizza and shoving it into his mouth.

"My cell phone is on in case you need anything," Miles told Crystal.

"I remember. And I have your date's number, too. And your parents'. We'll be fine. I have a lot of experience. I babysit all the time and I haven't had a problem yet."

He managed not to smile at the fourteen-year-old's bravado.

"Then I'll be seeing you."

Miles whistled as he jogged down the stairs and got into his car. Ordinarily he drove his SUV, but he'd washed and shined his sedan for this special occasion. As he neared Jillian's house, his heart sped up in excitement. It had only been a couple of days since he'd seen her, yet it seemed longer. When he parked and got out of the car, he took several deep breaths to steady himself and then sprinted up the stairs.

He rang the doorbell and looked around. Although the house and the resort were on the same property, the house was on a secluded piece of land, providing them all the privacy they could ever want.

He smiled as he envisioned bringing Jillian home that night and making good use of that privacy. Would she allow him to kiss her under the wide, dark sky? Or would she hustle him away as she scooted inside, leaving him standing alone in the cold?

He frowned. Why was he thinking of the end of the night when it hadn't even begun yet? They had hours of fun ahead of them and he intended to enjoy every single second.

"Come on in," Jillian said, swinging open the door. "I just need to grab my coat."

Dressed in a red sequined gown that caressed her slender curves, Jillian looked good enough to eat. In fact, she looked so sexy that all Miles could do was think of how much he wanted to undress her.

"You look absolutely beautiful."

"Thank you."

"And this is for you," he said, handing her the chocolate.

"My favorites." She shimmied a happy dance that made him smile even as it filled him with desire.

"I remember."

"I'm going to save these for later." She set the box on the coffee table.

"This is for you, too," he said, offering her the corsage.

She opened the container and smiled in delight at the pink and white orchids.

"Do you need help putting it on?" he asked, hoping she'd say yes.

Jillian nodded.

Their fingers brushed as Miles took the flowers from her hand. He stepped closer and got a whiff of Jillian's light perfume. Slipping his hand beneath the silky fabric of her dress, he was zapped by the heat from Jillian's skin. She was so soft, so warm and his fingers ached to caress her. His breathing became labored and it took supreme effort to concentrate on the task at hand. After a minute of sweet agony, he managed to secure the corsage to the thin strap of Jillian's dress.

"Thank you," she murmured, her voice barely above a whisper. Her fingers trembled as she touched her corsage. Their eyes met. Held. Sexual tension arced between them. They stood motionless for several long seconds. Then Jillian blinked and looked away.

He blew out a frustrated breath and then reminded himself that he was playing the long game. He knew it wouldn't be that easy to win back Jillian's love. But tonight was a big step toward convincing Jillian to give him—give *them*—a second chance.

He helped her with her coat and then held the front door for her. He wrapped his arm around her shoulder as they walked down the stairs to his car. Once they were safely ensconced inside, he turned on the radio to a station that played the latest pop and soul hits. Bruno Mars' latest song came over the air and Jillian began to sing along.

Although she hadn't been blessed with a spectacular voice, Jillian had always loved singing. She didn't care whether or not she was on key, which was good because she rarely was. For her, it had always been about enjoying herself, and she'd sung with gusto. Miles, on the other hand, had a great voice. As a child he'd lacked her confidence and had never sung alone in public. Now, though, he harmonized with her.

She stopped singing, turned and stared at him. "Wow. When did you start singing around people? You never do that. At least not by yourself. Even around me."

"You're confusing the new Miles with the old Miles." He'd gained his confidence when Benji had insisted that Miles sing a lullaby to him each night.

"I liked the old Miles, as you call him. Of course, the new Miles is growing on me."

"That's good to know."

The drive to the hotel passed quickly as they sang and laughed. Before long they were in Aspen Creek. When they reached the hotel, he joined the line of luxury cars waiting to park. Aspen Creek was an incredibly wealthy community filled with the haves and the have-mores. There was no wrong side of the tracks in this town. After Miles exchanged his car keys for a valet ticket, he and Jillian went inside.

A string quartet played softly, their music filling the air. The lobby had been decorated for the holiday with large urns of red and white roses on every surface. The crystal chandeliers provided glittery light. After checking their coats, they went into the ballroom that had been set up for dinner. Roses in crystal vases covered every possible surface. No expense had been spared.

Miles placed his hand on the small of Jillian's back as he led her through the maze of tables and chairs to where their friends awaited. He held her chair for her and then sat beside her. Glancing around, he noticed that they'd drawn quite a bit of attention.

She'd noticed the same thing. "Everyone is staring at us."

"I know." Aspen Creek was a small town where everyone had a passing acquaintance with their neighbors' business. It looked like he and Jillian were about to be featured in the next round of gossip. *Great.*

"I don't want people to get the wrong idea about us," she whispered, leaning near him. Her sweet scent teased him, momentarily distracting him.

"I think they have the right idea."

"What's that?"

"They're thinking that I'm the luckiest man on the planet to be accompanying the magnificent Jillian Adams."

She smiled. "When you put it like that, I guess you are pretty lucky."

He returned her smile. "Does that mean that I should buy another raffle ticket?"

"Absolutely. It's for a good cause after all. But don't expect to win. I mean, how lucky can one guy get?"

"True." But then, he didn't need to win the raffle. Just being with Jillian was prize enough.

He could have stared into her deep brown eyes all night, but they weren't alone. Erica approached and said something in Jillian's ear, and she turned away to respond. He felt a nudge on his shoulder and turned to look into Isaac's smirking face. His brother leaned in and whispered, "So, you and Jillian are back together again. I take it that she is no longer pissed that you didn't want to marry her before."

Miles whispered furiously, "We aren't together in the way you mean, and I don't want to talk about this here."

"So you aren't going to whip out a ring and propose to her tonight."

"Absolutely not." He looked over his shoulder to be sure that Jillian hadn't heard him. The last thing he wanted was to scare her away. She was jittery enough about being with him again. Even a casual mention of marriage could set his plan back. When she laughed at something her friend said, Miles continued. "I'll gladly stand guard if you want to propose to your date."

"Funny," Isaac replied. "I'll leave family life to you."

Miles had been pulling his brother's chain. Isaac was a player who believed variety was the spice of life. But Miles had managed to shut him up. He didn't want to talk to his brother. He could do that any day of the week whether he wanted to or not. But conversation with Jillian was a rare commodity. She finished talking with Erica and smiled up at him, once more giving him her full attention.

Isaac must have still felt like being annoying, because he immediately asked Jillian a question. Miles wasn't amused, and he stepped on his brother's foot as hard as he could. Isaac winced but otherwise gave no indication that his toes were being smashed. In fact, he even smiled. Miles added even more pressure and narrowed his eyes, sending his brother a clear message: *Knock it off.* Either Isaac decided to have mercy on him, or his foot was aching, because he nodded and directed his attention to his own date.

Miles then turned back to Jillian. She winked

and he knew that she'd witnessed the interplay between them. He shook his head. "He can be so annoying."

"Like he's getting paid."

Miles agreed. "I don't want to talk about my brother."

"What do you want to talk about?"

"You. Have I told you how absolutely stunning you are?"

"Yes, but feel free to repeat yourself. I can never hear that too often. I took one look and knew this dress would be perfect for tonight."

"The dress is nice. You've always looked good in red. But I wasn't talking about your clothes. I was talking about you, Jillian. You are stunning."

The color rose on Jillian's cheeks, and she flashed him a smile. "Are you flirting with me?"

"I suppose I am. What do you think about that?"

"I think you must be under the influence of Valentine's Day. All of the romance around us is getting to you. The back-to-back love songs that the musicians are playing. The sweet scent of the flowers perfuming the air. The romantic light shimmering from the chandeliers paired with the right amount of candlelight. The delicious food that we're enjoying. The entire atmosphere is designed to put you in the mood for love and you're getting swept away."

"You might be right, but I'm not convinced that those things are the reason I'm feeling this way. It's all you, Jillian. It's always been you."

Chapter Thirteen

It's always been you. Miles's words echoed through Jillian's mind and her heart began to pound. Inhaling deeply, she forced herself not to take his words too seriously. She hadn't been kidding when she'd said that Miles was under the influence of the atmosphere. It was powerful. Unlike him, she was clearheaded. Besides, she recalled that she and Miles had been down this road before, and it hadn't ended well for her. Or to be fair, for him, either.

She didn't know what to say, but fortunately he didn't seem to be looking for a response. It was as if he'd simply wanted to say the words. Now that he'd dropped that bomb, he was ready to move on. It took some effort, but she managed to banish the words to the recesses of her mind where they belonged and stay in the moment.

While they ate, Miles regaled her with tales of life on the ranch. He talked about training his latest horse, something she knew he enjoyed immensely. She'd always loved watching him work with his horses. He had always been so patient and kind, leading them with gentle hands and a soft voice. He'd claimed to be better with animals than he was with people, but Jillian hadn't believed that for a minute. He'd always known how to talk to her. Equally important, he'd known how to listen.

After dessert and coffee, the mayor took the stage and made a brief speech, thanking everyone for their donations to the Aspen Creek Angels. The money raised would support charities in the state as well as youth programs in town.

When he finished speaking, a large crystal punch bowl filled with raffle tickets was placed on a table in the middle of the room. A hush fell over the crowd as he reached in and pulled out the winning ticket. Jillian wanted to support the cause, so she'd bought one. It hadn't made sense to try to win a weekend at her family's resort, so she'd given the ticket to Veronica.

Mayor Harrison held up the ticket for everyone to see. Ever the showman, he read slowly, pausing between each number in order to ramp up the suspense. When he'd read the final number, there was a happy cry from one of the waitresses. Holding her ticket in the air, she hurried to the mayor. They compared numbers and then he congratulated her.

"Well, that was fun," Jillian said.

"What do you mean *was*?" Miles asked. "The night is young. We haven't even gotten to the dancing portion of the evening."

The idea of dancing with Miles was tantalizing. Just the thought of being held in his arms was heavenly. Leaning her head against his chest would be pure bliss. Suddenly she was tired of playing it safe. It was Valentine's Day after all. Just for tonight she would let her heart be free and enjoy herself to the fullest. She could be sensible tomorrow. But tonight? Tonight she would lean into the fantasy and the romance of the setting.

The string quartet that had played quietly during dinner had been replaced by a DJ who was currently spinning an up-tempo record. Jillian began to tap her foot.

"Are you fine to stay? You aren't worried about Benji?"

"No." He grinned. "I hired an experienced babysitter. Are you worried about Lilliana?"

She shook her head.

"Then there's nothing stopping us. Let's hit the dance floor. I've got some new moves to show you."

Jillian couldn't help but smile at his enthusiasm. Miles had always been quiet, preferring listening to speaking, watching to being the center of attention. Except when it came to dancing. Once the music started, he became a different person.

Jillian took his outstretched hand and allowed him to lead her to the dance floor. She would have been happy to remain on the edge of the crowd, but Miles didn't stop walking until they were in the middle of the floor. He pulled her close and the heat from his body wrapped around her. "Try to keep up with me." He winked and then spun her around.

"When has that ever been a problem for me?"

He did a few fancy steps, closing the distance between them. "Times change. People change. Abilities change."

She shimmied her shoulders and swung her hips in a motion designed to gain his attention. When she saw the gleam in his eyes, she smiled confidently. "Maybe, but I still have it."

"Yeah, you do."

They danced to two fast songs, leaving Jillian exhilarated. She and Miles had always been in sync on the dance floor, not needing words to communicate. When the second fast song merged into a slow one, she instantly went into his arms. She leaned against him, closed her eyes and relaxed. She inhaled and got a whiff of his cologne. It had teased her while they'd eaten, playing on the edges of her senses. Now it surrounded her.

A nice-smelling man had always been her weakness and she sighed with contentment. He held her tight in his arms as they swayed together, slowly moving to the music. It was as if everyone else vanished, leaving the two of them alone in the world. If it were up to her, she and Miles would never leave the dance floor. Instead they'd bask in the serenity they'd found here.

As one song bled into the next, Jillian allowed herself to play *what if.* What if tonight marked a new beginning for her and Miles? What if Miles was sincerely interested in her? What if she allowed herself to fall in love with him again?

What if she was only deluding herself again? What if she was setting herself up for heartbreak? She stiffened and immediately Miles's arms loosened.

"What's wrong? Was I holding you too tight?"

It would be so easy to let him believe that. Much more preferable than letting him know she'd given herself a panic attack. "No. I'm not sure what happened, actually."

He raised an eyebrow. The song had come to an end, so mercifully they didn't draw curious stares. "Come on. Let's get a drink and sit down for a couple of minutes."

Jillian nodded and walked beside him as they left the dance floor. Several people stopped them as they walked off the floor to compliment them on their dancing. After grabbing flutes of champagne from a passing waiter, they found a secluded nook where they were guaranteed privacy.

They sat on a plush love seat, sipping the cool champagne and staring out the window. Twinkling white lights illuminated the patio, creating a romantic setting for those brave enough to endure the cold night. A young couple, dressed only in their evening finery and clearly enamored with each other, strolled along the stone patio. The man had taken off his suit jacket and the young woman was wearing it over her dress. Just looking at them made Jillian shiver.

Miles saw her and smiled. "Perhaps you shouldn't watch them."

"It's like a car wreck. I can't pull my eyes away."

Miles looked out the window at the couple, who were now in a serious clench, and then back to Jillian. "Do I make you uncomfortable?"

Without thinking, Jillian shook her head. "Of course not. Why would you even ask that?"

"Because something is obviously going on with you. I don't know what happened while we were dancing, but something went wrong. I have a feeling it has something to do with me."

"Because you're the center of the universe."

He blew out a breath and ran his hand over his neatly trimmed black hair. He usually wore a cowboy hat and seeing him without one was a rare treat. "Because we were enjoying ourselves. Everything was right between us. Then you stiffened. Since no-body said anything to you, I deduced that I'm the reason for your change of mood. That I did some-thing to upset you. Was I wrong?"

"Yes and no."

"Talk about hedging your bets."

"I don't want to discuss it."

"Fair enough. What would you like to do?"

She stood and held out her hand. "I need to make a pit stop in the ladies' room and then I want to dance. No talking or trying to figure things out. Just dancing."

"That sounds good to me. I'll be waiting right here for you."

Relief coursed through Miles as he watched Jillian walk away. He didn't know what had hap-pened, but he had a feeling that he'd been on shaky ground for a minute there. Luckily he'd managed to get them back on even footing again. But he knew they couldn't stay in limbo forever. He needed to make a move. He just wished he knew what direc-tion to take.

"Just what do you think you're doing?"

Miles turned toward the angry voice and found himself staring into the furious eyes of Jillian's brother Marty. Miles and Marty had never been friends, although they'd gotten along. That is until Miles had broken up with Jillian. Then Marty had made it plain that Miles was persona non grata. If he didn't want to marry Jillian, he had better stay away from her. He hadn't cared that Miles had only wanted time to figure out if she was the one. That he'd been trying to protect Jillian.

"I'm waiting on your sister. And then we're going to dance." He knew that wasn't what Marty meant, but he wasn't in the mood to explain himself to the other man. What happened between Miles and Jillian was between *Miles and Jillian*.

"You're not nearly as amusing as you think you are," Marty said, stepping closer. He'd changed out of his chef whites and into a suit now that the dinner portion of the evening had ended. He loomed over Miles, so Miles rose, standing to his full height of six foot four, silently communicating that he wasn't going to be intimidated.

Marty had always been popular with everyone, hence his nickname, Party Marty, so why was he harassing Miles instead of charming some woman out of her clothes?

"So are you planning on proposing marriage?"

"That's none of your business."

"You think not? Because I remember my sister being so sure you were going to ask her to marry you before. And I remember how heartbroken she was when you ended things. I was the one who was there, holding her as she cried her eyes out. Standing helpless when she tried to get over the pain by marrying someone she shouldn't have. I don't want to have to do that again."

"I don't want you to have to do that, either."

"Well, make sure you don't lead her on again. For a reason known only to her, Jillian has found you worthy of her love. But if you break her heart a second time, I'm not going to be happy. And trust, I'm going to focus that unhappiness in your direction."

Marty must have felt he'd sufficiently threatened Miles because he turned and stalked back into the ballroom, leaving Miles alone with his thoughts. He knew he wasn't good enough for Jillian. But then, nobody was. She was a shining star in a dark world. A goddess among mortals.

He heard her footsteps as she returned, a bright smile on her beautiful face. "Ready for more dancing?" she asked as she drew near.

Everything inside him yearned to say yes, but Marty's words had hit their mark. And Miles recalled the way that Jillian had reacted to him earlier when he'd told her that she was the one for him. How uncomfortable she'd seemed.

There was also the way she'd been on the dance floor. She'd been enjoying herself before she'd pulled back. Clearly she was afraid of being hurt. Afraid of trusting him with her feelings. She didn't believe that he was sincere. Words would never convince her. Only his actions over time would. More time than tonight. The worst thing would be for him to do a full-on blitz which could result in her feeling pressured. He didn't want to move faster than she was comfortable doing.

What was the hurry? After all, this was their first date and he'd had to work hard to convince her to come with him. He might want to take their relationship to the next level, but she was still adjusting to being friends. It would be unfair not to give her space and time to figure out what kind of relationship she wanted to have with him.

But he didn't trust himself to maintain his distance if he had her in his arms again. He was holding on to his control by a thread.

But since Jillian was nervous, he was going to slow down, no matter how much he hated the idea. After all, he'd taken time in the past to be sure that Jillian was the right one for him. She deserved the same opportunity now. "No. Let's sit here a minute. I want to talk."

She inhaled deeply and very slowly blew out the breath. "Why do I get the feeling that I'm not going to like what you're going to say?"

He placed his hands on her shoulders. "I feel like we need to slow things down."

"What things?" She shook her head and took a giant step away from him. "What happened? Everything was fine until I went to touch up my makeup. Did someone say something to you? Was your brother giving you grief about us? I know how he likes to tease you."

She was close. He was tempted to set the record straight by mentioning that it was *her* brother who'd given him pause, but he wouldn't. Jillian adored Marty and Miles would never do anything to interfere with that relationship. Besides, Marty had been right. Jillian's comfort and peace of mind needed to come first. She had been hurt before. By him. She deserved time to decide her next move without the pressure of his presence. He'd already let her know that he wanted to be with her. Now he had to give her the opportunity to see if she wanted the same thing.

"No, he didn't say a word. It's just that things are happening really quickly between us. It's easy to fall into old habits because they're comfortable. You're right, the atmosphere is affecting us and we're in danger of being swept away. We need to be sure that we're acting on what we feel for real and not being influenced by everything around us."

She shook her head. "Unbelievable. You're unbelievable. You know, I wasn't even going to come to this stupid dance, but you insisted that it would be fun. And it was. Until now."

"It still can be." He hadn't made himself clear so he inhaled so he could start over. He wanted to let her know that he would wait until she was comfortable with being more than friends.

"Save it." She turned to walk away, and he touched her hand, stopping her.

"Where are you going?"

"I'm going back to the dance. My parents left earlier, but my brothers are in there. I'm sure one of them will give me a ride home."

"Don't do that, Jillian. We can still dance. And I can do a better job of explaining myself."

She rolled her eyes and gave a harsh laugh. "I don't want to dance with you. And you've said quite enough."

"Okay. Then I'll take you home." This hadn't gone the way he'd planned. Maybe they could clear the air in the car.

She shook her head. "I'll catch a ride with Marty."

There was nothing he could say to dissuade her, but as he watched her walk away, he had a sinking feeling that he'd just made another huge mistake in their relationship. Sadly, there was no way to undo it this time, either.

"I can't believe I started to fall for him again," Jillian said to Marty as they drove home. She'd been raging since they'd left the hotel, alternating between anger at Miles and at herself. Anything to keep the pain at bay. "You must think I'm the stupidest person in the world."

"Why would I think something like that?"

"Because I keep doing the same thing over again

and hoping for a different result. When I came back home, I told myself to stay away from him. And I had planned to do that. Then Benji and Lilliana ended up in the same playgroup and we were thrown together. I tried to keep my distance, but it wasn't that easy. And I found myself liking him again. And heaven help me, Marty, but I think I fell in love with him again."

Marty only glanced at her and then back out the windshield. Since he didn't say anything, she continued. "And fool that I am, I thought that he was starting to fall in love with me, too. He's the one who wanted to go to the dance together. I was perfectly happy staying home."

"Is that right?"

"Well, maybe not happy, but I would have gotten over it. We were having a great time together. I should have never gone to touch up my makeup. Because he was completely different when I got back. He went from planning to dance the night away to spewing some nonsense about slowing down. It wouldn't hurt so much if it hadn't been so unexpected."

Marty was silent. Too silent. She loved her brother, but he had an opinion on everything and was not shy about sharing it. Not only that, he had a tendency to be very protective where she was concerned. She turned and stared at him. "What did you do?"

"What makes you think I did anything?"

The non-answer. "Come on, Marty. I know you. And please, I don't need a second man treating me like I'm a child in need of protection."

"You do need protecting." His voice was firm. He'd gone from being her pal—the brother she'd always had fun with and was closest to—to being her big brother. Her guardian.

"From you?"

"Of course not. I would never hurt you."

"Then tell me what you did."

Marty grimaced and squeezed the steering wheel. "I told him that he'd better not hurt you again."

"Is that all?" Miles wouldn't back away from a simple warning.

Marty frowned. They'd reached her parents' house and he parked and started to get out of the car. She grabbed his arm, holding him in place. "What else did you say?"

"Nothing important."

"Who are you protecting? Me or you?"

"I don't need protecting."

"I wouldn't be so sure of that. What. Else. Did. You. Say?"

He heaved out a breath. "I asked him about his intentions."

"Marty." She narrowed her eyes. "And what else?"

"And nothing. That's it. That's the gist of it."

Her heart ached as she realized what Miles must

have said. What Marty was avoiding telling her. "He didn't give you the answer you wanted, so you scared him away from me."

"Jillian—"

"It doesn't matter, Marty. Miles and I have been very clear that we are only friends. I'm the one who forgot so I'm the one to blame. Don't be mad at him because my feelings are hurt."

"I'll be mad at whomever I choose."

Jillian shook her head. There was no getting her brother to listen to reason. But she loved him, so she'd let it pass. She couldn't even be angry at him for butting in. He'd only saved her from herself. If he hadn't put an end to the relationship, she would probably have fallen more deeply in love with Miles than she was now. And eventually she'd end up in even more pain.

It was for the best, she reminded herself. If only she could make herself believe it.

Chapter Fourteen

"So, are you going to tell me what's bugging you?" Isaac asked Miles a week later

"What makes you think something is on my mind?" He looked up before taking another step around the corral. He was in the early stages of training Beauty. The filly was getting used to being led around by the rope around her neck. Training horses was something he enjoyed but his brother's questioning was putting a damper on that pleasure.

Miles was doing his best to avoid giving an answer. He was getting pretty good at doing that. Probably because he was getting lots of practice. Benji had been asking him about Lily and Jilly, as he called them, for the past three days. Jillian hadn't brought Lilliana to playgroup this week and Benji missed them. He wasn't the only one. They'd already planned to meet up with the kids at the children's museum this Saturday. Jillian hadn't called to cancel, so he believed that she would still be coming. At least he hoped she would. Benji didn't need more disappointment.

"Don't play stupid games with me, please. Just answer the question."

"If you must know, it's Benji."

"What's wrong with him? He isn't sick, is he?"

"No. He just misses Lilliana and Jillian." There was a lot of that going around.

His brother leaned against the fence, putting his booted foot on the bottom rail. Isaac had stopped by to let him know that he would be out of town for a few days. He'd gotten a cryptic message from a lawyer and was on his way to Chicago. His plane left in a few hours.

"Trouble in paradise?"

"Paradise? Jillian and I weren't in a relationship. We were just friends."

"You don't really think I believe that, do you?"

"You should. It's the truth." A painful truth he was having a hard time accepting. Especially since it appeared that their friendship was over.

"Then what has been going on with you? What was Valentine's Day all about? You guys couldn't keep your eyes off of each other at dinner or your hands off each other on the dance floor. I half expected you to say that you were getting engaged."

That stopped Miles in his tracks. "Why would you say something like that?"

"Because I have eyes in my head. I might not know everything there is to know about love, except to avoid it at all costs, but even I know what I saw between you and Jillian."

"And that was?" Miles asked, even though he wasn't sure he wanted to know. He didn't want to get his hopes up.

"That you love that woman. And she loves you."

Miles wished Isaac was right, yet he knew his brother was wrong. Jillian had said she wasn't looking for love. She'd proved that when she hadn't responded when Miles said she was the one. It had been as if she was hoping the moment would pass without her having to tell Miles she didn't love him. Even so, he couldn't help but ask, "You think Jillian loves me?"

"Of course. Don't you?"

He hadn't dared to hope. Jillian's obvious fear of being hurt had made him cautious. Perhaps too cautious. He just didn't want to take things too fast when she was obviously skittish.

"You're looking a little bit green there, Miles," Isaac said. His voice was a mixture of concern and mockery. "Surely I'm not telling you anything you don't already know."

"It's not what I expected to hear. Jillian is so unsure around me. She'll be enjoying herself and then she'll withdraw, as if she's afraid I'll let her down again."

"Do you blame her?"

"No. That's why I told Jillian that we needed to slow things down."

"Again?" Isaac shook his head in disgust.

"I thought I was relieving the pressure and giving her time to feel comfortable with me again."

Isaac simply kept shaking his head.

"What?"

"What was the point? You know how she feels about you. How she's always felt about you. And you went and made a mess of this. I've got a plane to catch. You stop wasting time with that horse and figure out how you're going to make things better before you lose her again."

With that, Isaac left, leaving Miles feeling worse than he had before. He didn't want to hurt Jillian. He'd been trying to give her space. Time to feel comfortable moving from friendship to romance. He'd been trying to do the right thing. But he'd ended up causing her pain.

And she wasn't the only one he'd hurt. Benji had been moping around ever since Lilliana and Jillian hadn't shown up for playgroup. If Miles had thought his son would forget about them easily, he'd only been kidding himself. They were a big part of his son's life.

"Daddy?"

Miles turned at Benji's voice. "Yeah, bud?"

"Is today the day we go to the museum and see Lily and Jilly?"

Benji had asked him that question several times a day and each time Miles had needed to give him a negative answer. Benji's shoulders had sunk, breaking Miles's heart and making him feel even guiltier about how he'd handled things with Jillian. She had neither asked nor needed him to protect her.

"Is it daddy?"

Miles smiled. "Yes. Today is the day. Are you ready?"

Benji smiled. "I'm going to hug Lily and Jilly really tight when I see them."

"Me, too." Or at least he wanted to. He would have to see how things went with Jillian.

After his talk with his brother, Miles had begun to plan on the best way to let Jillian know he wanted to be with her forever. And what said forever better than a diamond engagement ring?

He patted his pocket, assuring himself that the three-carat solitaire that he'd bought was still there.

"Are we going to get some hot chocolate and ride on the train?"

"If that's what you want."

Benji nodded enthusiastically.

Benji chattered the entire time Miles drove to town, but Miles was too preoccupied to follow the conversation closely. He must have made all the right comments because Benji didn't complain once on the ride to the children's museum. Benji was thrilled to be hanging out with Lilliana and his head was on a swivel as he looked around the building for her. Miles and Benji were a bit early so they had to wait a few minutes.

"When will Lily be here?" Benji asked.

"Soon."

"How long is that?"

Miles shrugged. He couldn't blame Benji for being excited when he felt the same. He talked to the teenage boy running the train, handed him a bag and gave him final instructions. The teenager smiled and nodded.

"How about you take a train ride while we wait?" Miles asked Benji.

"Without Lily?" The idea didn't appeal to Benji who shook his head.

"Okay. Then we should get out of the way so other kids can get on. I'll text Jillian to let her know where we are." Miles sent the quick message and then took Benji's hand. Benji looked around again, and then froze.

"What's wrong?"

Benji grinned and then pointed. "They're here." He didn't wait to see if Miles was following before he raced away.

"Oh. I see." Miles strode behind his son. When he caught up to him, Benji and Lilliana were hugging.

"Look, Daddy. It's Lily and Jilly," Benji exclaimed. The smile that had been missing had reappeared on his little boy's face.

Benji and Lilliana looked positively delighted to be with each other. Benji hadn't been this happy in days. Truth be told, Miles was feeling better than he'd felt since he'd ruined Valentine's Day. It was as if his heart had been broken and was now trying to knit itself together.

Jillian was standing a couple of feet behind Lilliana, watching the reunion, a somber expression on her face. He knew that he was the reason that she wasn't smiling. Hopefully he could change that.

"Up," Lilliana demanded, coming to stand in front of Miles.

Miles smiled and complied, lifting the little girl into his arms and giving her a quick hug before settling her on his shoulders. He didn't realize how much he'd missed her until he felt her slight weight. After a moment, he lowered her down to stand beside Benji and then looked at Jillian. Though she'd greeted Benji with a warm hug and a kiss on his cheek, her eyes were distant when she looked at him.

He didn't blame her. If she'd been falling in love with him, she would want to do everything in her power to protect her heart. Especially if she held the mistaken belief that he didn't love her. He wanted to protect her heart, too. It was just that his best effort had blown up in his face, hurting both of them. Though she was doing her best not to look at him, he saw the pain in her eyes. And it broke his heart.

"Daddy, Lily and I want to ride on the train," Benji said.

"Is it okay with you, Jillian?" he asked.

"Of course. I brought Lilliana here so that she could have fun."

"That's the same reason I brought Benji. He's been miserable these past few days. He really misses you and Lilliana."

Jillian nodded. The kids had started walking in the direction of the train station and Jillian fell in behind them. He watched her walk away, momentarily distracted by the gentle sway of her hips, before he stirred himself and jogged to catch up with them. Once the kids were on the train, Miles touched Jillian's hand to get her attention.

"I wonder if we could talk?"

She blew out a breath. "I think we've done quite enough talking as it is. And to be honest, there's not much you can say that I'm interested in hearing."

"I understand. But please, let me apologize. I'm sorry for ruining Valentine's Day."

She scoffed. "You're worried about a dance."

"No. That doesn't cover it. But that's where things fell apart."

"Miles, don't worry about it. I understand. We were falling into old habits even though I knew better. My biggest regret is how this has affected Lilliana. I should have never allowed her to become so attached to you and Benji. She's missed you both."

"I don't think you had much of a say in how that turned out. They loved each other instantly."

"Still, after that first day, I shouldn't have taken her back to play group. I know how you are and knew that we would end up here. I was just foolish to think you were different now. I should have known that nobody changes that much."

"I have changed."

"I know you think that, and that's what makes this all so sad. You thought it was fine for us to be together until Marty scared you away."

"Marty told you that?"

"No. I guessed. Your about-face was too abrupt to have come from inside you. Just know that I'm not the same girl who was desperately in love with you and didn't know how to handle your rejection."

"You've got it all wrong, Jillian."

She slammed her hands on her hips. Her eyes flashed in anger. She was glorious. "What did I get wrong?"

"Everything. I didn't back up because Marty scared me away. I did it for you."

"For me?"

"Yes. I could tell you were scared. I sensed it when we danced. Even before then, when I said it's always been you in my heart. I knew I'd come on too strong and that I was rushing you. You didn't believe my feelings. Didn't trust them. Perhaps because you didn't trust your own. I knew you needed time and space to deal with your feelings Time to believe mine."

"But Marty…"

"Do you think I'm scared of your brother? I'm not. But talking to him reminded me that I'd taken time in the past to be sure that our relationship was right. You deserved the same opportunity to be comfortable. To be sure. That's what I was trying to do."

"Oh."

"Yeah. Oh."

"I'm not sure what you're saying to me, Miles. I don't want to misread the situation. But I want you to know that whether you love me or whether you don't, I'll be fine."

Miles only stared at her. Clearly she'd shocked him. Heck, she'd surprised herself there, too. But what she'd said was true. She might love Miles— something she hadn't said—but her life would go on happily without him. She wouldn't go off the deep end and marry the wrong person as she'd done years ago.

"So, are you saying you love me?" he asked.

"That's not what I said at all." In fact, she'd been careful *not* to say that. If she did say *that* he might say the same in order to protect her. She didn't want him to say he loved her unless it was true. Her heart didn't need his protection. It needed his honesty.

"So you're saying you *don't* love me."

Jillian shook her head. Miles could be so aggravating. "What difference does it make? You don't love me." The words were painful, but maybe she needed to feel that pain to face the truth.

"Who told you that?"

"You did."

"Jillian, I never once in my life said I didn't love you."

"I'm not going to play semantics. You might love me, but you're not in love with me."

"That's not true."

Her heart skipped a beat, but she ignored it. She wasn't going to be misled. "Since when?"

"Since forever."

She held up a hand in front of her. This needed to stop. "Don't."

"I know I messed up before, but I won't again. I love you, Jillian. I want to be with you."

"No. You don't get to say that. If you want to talk, you need to tell the truth."

He looked so flustered. So annoyed with himself.

So Miles. "That's just it. I am." He rubbed a hand over his chin. "I'm sorry, Jillian. For everything."

"For what? And for when? Hurting me before or hurting me now?"

"Both. They're one and the same thing." He looked around the museum and she did the same. The train would be returning soon.

"You said you wanted to see other people to be sure that what we felt was real."

"Yes. But that didn't just mean me. That meant you, too. I wanted to be sure that you loved me as much as you said you did. I guess I wasn't confident enough to believe in our love. Especially your love for me."

"Well, Miles. I did love you. There are no words to express how badly you hurt me."

"I know. And I can never express how sorry I am for that."

She shrugged. "It doesn't matter now, Miles. The past is over and can't be changed. I have put it behind me and now I'm looking toward the future."

"Me, too."

"Really? Because it seems to me that you're behaving the same way that you did in the past. Not saying what you really mean. Running away."

"I wasn't running this time. But I saw how nervous I made you. I thought that backing away was the wise choice."

"Things were moving very quickly," Jillian admitted. If he could be honest about his doubts, she could, too.

"And we have two children to think about. Although to be honest, I don't think they'll have a problem adjusting."

"Adjusting to what?"

"To us being together."

Her heart stuttered. "What are you talking about?"

"I'm talking about us. Getting married. The way we should have years ago."

Jillian's heart sank in disappointment. She'd dreamed of Miles proposing to her for so many years. In her mind there'd been flowers and a romantic candlelit dinner. Not them standing in the middle of the children's museum and him casually throwing out the idea as if it were suggesting they get cotton candy. As if getting married was nothing big. It was so cut-and-dried. So bloodless. Like a business deal that only required a handshake to be completed.

"Is this your idea of a joke?"

He blinked as if surprised by her reaction. "No. I'm one hundred percent serious."

"Really? This is the best you can do?" She waved her arms around, encompassing the entire setting. Kids were running around, some ignoring their parents who called their names. One kid was crying and yelling that he didn't want to go home now. The commotion, although not overwhelming, definitely wasn't candlelight and flowers.

He sighed and then stepped in front of her, preventing her from walking away. "I'm telling you that I love you with all of my heart. I'm saying that I want to marry you and create a family with us and our children. I'm asking you to take a chance on me. I promise everything will be different. I'll be different Because all I want is you. I know this isn't a fancy restaurant. I thought that might bring back bad memories. But we have made happy memories here. In this museum. Which is why I thought we could add one more happy memory."

He nodded and smiled at someone over her shoulder. She turned and gasped. The little children on the train were each holding a rose. Several little boys were waving their flowers. The teenager in charge of the train helped the kids climb from the train cars. One by one, they walked over to Jillian. Each child handed their rose to Jillian until she held nearly two dozen roses.

She looked around the room. Everyone had stopped what they were doing and were watching to see what would happen next. Jillian was wondering that, too.

Miles stood in front of her. "I love you, Jillian. I always have. And I always will."

She blinked as his words hit her. She heard the

sincerity there. The honesty. The love. And then the tears came. Happy tears.

Before she could reply, he knelt down and took her hands into his. "Jillian Marie Adams, will you do me the honor of being my wife? I promise I'll love you forever and do everything in my power to be sure you never have cause to doubt my love again."

Jillian's heart began pounding and she inhaled deeply, trying to slow it down. So many thoughts battled for control of her mind. She tried to order them so she could take them out and look at them before deciding, but they jumped around too much for her to grab on to more than one. The one that reminded her that she loved Miles and wanted to marry him. Fears from the past tried to stop her, but she shoved them down. It suddenly didn't matter that this wasn't the type of proposal she'd always dreamed of. Or that curious people were watching them attentively, a few directing phone cameras their way. What mattered was the man she'd always loved wanted to build a future with her.

She realized she'd been standing quietly for a long while when she saw the doubt begin to creep into Miles's eyes. It would be so easy to hurt him if she wasn't careful. Just as he'd hurt her. Not out of lack of love but out of carelessly spoken words. "Yes! Yes, I'll marry you, Miles."

He pulled a ring from his pocket and slipped it

onto her left ring finger. She glanced at it. Yowza! It was gorgeous. He jumped to his feet, lifted her in his arms and spun around in a circle. She laughed with joy as he set her on her feet and then, while she was still trying to grab her breath, he leaned his forehead against hers.

"I know I messed up in the past, but I promise the future will be so much better."

"I know."

Benji and Lilliana had been standing with the teen who ran the train. Now they stepped forward, smiles on their faces.

The two children were holding hands.

"Thank you for helping with the proposal," Miles said.

"My pleasure. Congratulations." He smiled and then dashed back over to the train station.

"Do you like the flowers, Jilly?" Benji asked.

"I do."

Lilliana hadn't handed over her flower. Now she was picking the petals off the rose and dropping them onto the floor.

"Why did you give Jilly flowers?" Benji asked. Miles and Jillian shared a glance. She nodded. Miles smiled. "I asked Jillian to marry me and be my wife. She said yes."

Benji simply stared at him. Clearly that meant nothing to him. But then he was only three.

Jillian knelt before the kids and took each of them

by the hand. "That means that Lilliana and I will be part of your family and you'll be part of ours. We'll live in the house with you and your daddy. Is that okay?"

Benji nodded and smiled. "I love Lily. And I love you, Jilly."

Jillian smiled. "I love you, too. And so does Lilliana."

"Are you happy, bud?" Miles asked.

Benji nodded. "Can we ride the train again?"

"Twain?" Lilliana echoed.

"Anything that makes you happy," Miles said. Then he brushed a quick kiss against Jillian's lips. "Same thing goes for you. I'll do anything to make you happy."

She smiled. She knew that. "I'm already happy. And I know with you by my side, I always will be."

"You've got that right. We're going to live happily ever after."

* * * * *

Look for Isaac's story,
The Rancher's Baby

The next installment in Aspen Creek Bachelors,
Kathy Douglass' new miniseries for
Harlequin Special Edition

On sale April 2023, wherever Harlequin
books and ebooks are sold!

#2965 FOR THE RANCHER'S BABY
Men of the West • by Stella Bagwell

Maggie Malone traveled to Stone Creek Ranch to celebrate her best friend's wedding—not fall in love herself! But ranch foreman Cordell Hollister is too charming and handsome to resist! When their fling ends with a pregnancy, will a marriage of convenience be enough for the besotted bride-to-be?

#2966 HOMETOWN REUNION
Bravo Family Ties • by Christine Rimmer

Sixteen years ago, Hunter Bartley left town to seek fame and fortune. Now the TV star is back, eager to reconnect with the woman he left behind...and the love he could never forget. But can JoBeth Bravo trust love a second time when she won't leave and he can never stay?

#2967 WINNING HER FORTUNE
The Fortunes of Texas: Hitting the Jackpot • by Heatherly Bell

Alana Searle's plan for one last hurrah before her secret pregnancy is exposed has gone awry! Her winning bachelor-auction date is *not* with one of the straitlaced Maloney brothers but with bad boy Cooper Fortune Maloney himself. What if her unexpected valentine is daddy material after all?

#2968 THE LAWMAN'S SURPRISE
Top Dog Dude Ranch • by Catherine Mann

Charlotte Pace is already overwhelmed with her massive landscaping job and caring for her teenage brother. Having Sheriff Declan Winslow's baby is just *too much*! But Declan isn't ready to let the stubborn, independent beauty forget their fling...nor the future they could have together.

#2969 SECOND TAKE AT LOVE
Small Town Secrets • by Nina Crespo

Widow Myles Alexander wants to renovate and sell his late wife's farmhouse—not be the subject of a Hollywood documentary. But down-to-earth director Holland Ainsley evokes long-buried feelings, and soon he questions everything he thought love could be. Until drama follows her to town, threatening to ruin everything...

#2970 THE BEST MAN'S PROBLEM
The Navarros • by Sera Taíno

Rafael Navarro thrives on routines and control. Until his sister recruits him to help best man Etienne Galois with her upcoming nuptials. Spontaneous and adventurous, Etienne seems custom-made to trigger Rafi's annoyance...and attraction. Can he face his surfacing feelings before their wedding partnership ends in disaster?

HARLEQUIN
PLUS

Try the best multimedia subscription service for romance readers like you!

Read, Watch and Play.

Experience the easiest way to get the romance content you crave.

Start your **FREE TRIAL** at
www.harlequinplus.com/freetrial.